IT'S NOT NOTHING

COURTNEY DENELLE

sfwp.com

Library of Congress Cataloging-in-Publication Data
Names: Denelle, Courtney, 1982- author.
Title: It's not nothing / Courtney Denelle.
Other titles: It is not nothing
Description: Santa Fe, NM : Santa Fe Writers Project, 2022. | Summary:
    "Rosemary Candwell's past has exploded into her present. Down-and-out
    and deteriorating, she drifts from anonymous beds and bars in
    Providence, to a homeless shelter hidden among the hedge-rowed avenues
    of Newport, and through the revolving door of service jobs and quick-fix
    psychiatric care, always grasping for hope, for a solution. She's
    desperate to readjust back into a family and a world that has deemed her
    a crazy bitch living a choice they believe she could simply un-choose at
    any time. She endures flashbacks and panic attacks, migraines and
    nightmares. She can't sleep or she sleeps for days; she lashes out at
    anyone and everyone, especially herself. She abuses over-the-counter
    cold medicine and guzzles down anything caffeinated just to feel less
    alone. What if her family is right? What if she is truly broken beyond
    repair? Drawn from the author's experience of homelessness and trauma
    recovery, It's Not Nothing is a collage of small moments, biting jokes,
    intrusive memories, and quiet epiphanies meant to reveal a greater
    truth: Resilience never looks the way we expect it to look"— Provided
    by publisher.
Identifiers: LCCN 2022005199 (print) | LCCN 2022005200 (ebook) |
    ISBN 9781951631239 (trade paperback) | ISBN 9781951631246 (ebook)
Subjects: LCGFT: Novels.
Classification: LCC PS3604.E535 I87 2022 (print) |
    LCC PS3604.E535 (ebook) | DDC 813/.6—dc23/eng/20220415
LC record available at https://lccn.loc.gov/2022005199
LC ebook record available at https://lccn.loc.gov/2022005200

Published by SFWP
369 Montezuma Ave. #350
Santa Fe, NM 87501
www.sfwp.com

For Bethany, my North Star

And it's inside myself that I must
create someone who will understand.

—Clarice Lispector

SUMMER

THE OLD INJURIES
SWELL WITHIN ME

Stories told and retold. They taste like blood in my mouth.

The doctors all say, Well said, and I swallow my contempt at their surprise. I resist the urge to tell them, Yes, of course. *Well said* is my thing. They have no way of knowing it's all I've got left, this describing the water as I drown.

Here I am treated with an exasperated sigh, a port in the arm meant to replenish, a bald turkey sandwich, and a plastic cup of apple juice. No one promises things will get better. No one says this too shall pass. Their only answer to having seen it all before is a neutrality of language with disdain vibrating just beneath the surface. It's just as well. Nothing can be promised to me now. I do not want it to be.

I'm curtained off and left alone, a picture of wrack and ruin. Is this relief that I am feeling or is this dread? Why not both, is what I venture. In that way, the end starts from here.

We had been stopped at the red light alongside Memorial Hospital when I saw them. Gray and withered, outfitted in papery johnnies, gathered together at the main entrance. Each had a cigarette in one hand, the slim pole of an IV drip in the other. Plastic tubes fastened to their arms. Automatic doors opened and closed behind them, a metronome marking time.

I was just a girl then, but the sight of them circling beneath their smoke cloud had conjured an absent feeling in me. Like a dream that reminded me of something I'd forgotten as opposed to a memory of the thing itself.

The dead take their secrets with them.

I don't have to see them to know they're out there. Revenants, all of them. Circling, circling—cast out but unable to cross over, tethered to life. I consider my options. How I could make my way out there and bum a smoke. How I could get out. How I could get on with it. How I could get away.

On the Incurable Ward, the door locked both ways. A door made of steel. But not here. I squeak and wobble down the hall, white-knuckling the IV drip by my side. The whispers at the nurses' station rise and fall as I pass.

There's the world you live in, then there's the previous state of the world the moment you choose to act. Actions and the extension of those actions. They are separate but intersecting circles.

MY DISSOCIATIVE IDENTITY WALKS INTO A BAR

Father's Day—what a scene! The whole bar teems with men who tried and failed, or just failed. All of them tying it on, trying to get on with it.

They open their mouths wide. They toss their heads back. They laugh like it costs them nothing to laugh as they do. Like it's directing them to some grander cultural goal. And he's out there somewhere, frantically wondering, Does she remember? She does.

I've taken cover in the stations of my own discarded life. Chasing a high time, holding court, I'm awash in the attention of drunks looking to get laid. I hide my backpack beneath my barstool. Out of sight. It's bursting at the seams with all that I have.

I hear my voice in introduction.

I'm Rosemary.

Am I?

A band plays. We, the audience, are not on their side. There's the sound guy who's also the bartender. There's the bellied-up regulars, the soon-to-be lifers, a lot of shitty, shitty men who ought to be thanking the band because now they've got something to bitch about. What I'm dying to ask them is, Was it really better back then or were you just younger?

It doesn't help that the band is, in fact, terrible. But most bands are terrible, just like most painters are terrible, and writers too. The difference is, writers and painters don't demand your attention. Our terrible doesn't involve a microphone.

The singer plugs another show between songs.

Come out and support, he says.

Support what—you? This?

I didn't always live like this. I used to live a different life.

It's a difference of being down and out versus the performance of down and out. Sure, I can feel the glares trained in my direction, can hear the whispers growing louder. But I pass—I think I pass. Navigating this *situation* within a community that romanticizes the suffering artist. Where one person's daily struggle is another person's passion project.

Dilettantes, dabbling in the dread of a mind gone dark. Their *authenticity*, a euphemism for the absence of an original idea.

Deep in my cups, I meet no strangers. The more it happens, the more predictable it becomes. Introductions include band names, whatever the hell band they played in ten years ago. So, what you do is, you start with the idea that most people are full of shit.

I am a guest star, younger than all of them. The age difference is no small thing, here on the fringe of fully formed friend groups. Those who have gone through the fires of their twenties together, coupling and un-coupling, collaborating, drinking, drugging, un-drugging, collaborating again, then intermittently ostracizing, coupling with some idea of permanence, going back to school, moving out of bad neighborhoods into somewhat better neighborhoods, moving on and, now, connecting with one another only through reminiscence, as if *we were young together* is all that's required to sustain a friendship.

Me? I'm a bridge-burner, myself.

I've never *not* been around. A true townie. Hell, we might have crossed paths before—whether I remember is another thing. But I am welcome as a spectator, as an extension of *him,* whomever I am linked to that night. We will talk about him, we will relate to one another through him, but we will never talk about me.

Which is fine. I say stuff like—I'd love to hear the story about the A&R guy who took your band out for dinner in '96!

What I never say is—good luck, you imbeciles, your nostalgia is killing you.

I have only myself to blame for withstanding this, taking it on the chin with these people. It's not to say there's no benefit for me.

A thing no one talks about is how you can wield a person by letting him think he's wielding you. I'm no grifter. I'm just taking the elevator down, all the way down.

The terrible drummer of the terrible band sidles up to me in the corner. And for the umpteenth time, I miss the chance to self-appoint a nickname.

I tell him he should've just played "Wipeout" for thirty minutes— give the people what they want. He scans me as I laugh, as if I'm laughing at his expense. But it's merely the hope of a private joke getting into the water supply, even if the private joke is between me and myself.

What do I *do?* Like—for money? What do I do for money, is that what you're asking? I make lattes and mixed drinks and sometimes art. Formerly. Now? I make a mess, is what I make. But I let him off easy and I follow him home. Because anyone who shows any interest, I follow them home.

The drummer woos me with mushrooms. I've been *saving* these, he says. And I'm honored, I guess?

It's a giggly trip, barely a trip. We watch *Mission: Impossible* on cable. He's convinced the whole thing is a Toyota commercial. He is easy to convince.

What's so funny? he asks.

It just kills me, I say, winded. Tom Cruise running.

In a fit of inspiration, I suggest he change the band name from whatever the hell to Monkey Knife Fight. You can have that, I tell him. I'm *giving* it to you.

There have been times I thought I was a genius. Now—not so much.

The sex is crime scene sex. I had balked, but he told me, no, no, no he was cool with it. The whole ordeal reeks like grimy pennies. I wonder if he wonders, was it worth it? Because now laundry has become a priority and, judging from the state of him and his bedroom, laundry has never been a priority.

A broke-ass period is, for me, all about paper towels; paper towels, lifted by the ream from the Convention Center bathroom because the mall has switched to hand-dryers in an effort to be green.

What's the thing about bears and menstruation? Is it the blood they're drawn to or the pheromones?

Mauled by a bear, ripped to shreds, ripped to death—I'm not lining up for it or anything, but it has its appeal. I'd like to be taken out by something mightier than me. I've had the same thought, night swimming and drunk. I would swim out far, too far, content to be taken by the ocean. I'd be honored.

This way I'm headed, this way I've gone, it will probably be something pathetic that does me in. Like I'll be struck and killed by a Smart Car. Or, worse, struck by a Smart Car, surviving but dying slowly, knowing I was smote by a fucking Smart Car.

I've tried to end it on my own terms. Believe you me. I failed and I failed and I failed and I failed.

Me and Myself are approached by a bear.

Myself takes off running.

Me says, What the hell are you doing? You can't outrun a bear!

Myself says, Bitch, I only have to outrun *you*.

The gathering dark, it gathers around me. I am the body to which it is drawn.

And yet—what do I know of bodies? Me, a ghost trapped in this rotting meat machine.

But no more old bastards. Tell them to fuck off. Tell them to go to hell. Take the free drink, and then tell them to fuck all the way off.

No more old bastards after this old bastard. He's ugly, that's for sure. His mouth is one of those small, thin-lipped mouths. Like someone kicked a hole in a paper bag. He's got no money. He's also an idiot. The appeal with this Old Bastard is, I'm not getting out alive. I'm gonna take this one straight to the rockiest of bottoms. *Finally.*

In terms of viability, my life has no inherent value, so—

He's two weeks out from having a seizure. Delirium tremens, like you read about. This is information he leads with! He's evangelical in his denial, desperate to convince. He tells me how he got fired from his bartending gig, how he's stuck making sandwiches at a café down by the hospital. Some bars won't serve him anymore, not even the real rat hole dives he's patronized for years. And I get it. No one wants to meet themself in this Old Bastard's consequences. They told him to hit bricks, as if they were looking out for him, like they were doing him a favor.

People're making a big deal outta nothing, he says. I'm just a party boy.

Party boy? But you're, what, forty-five?

As one peels away from the bar, then another, then another, this Old Bastard yells out all in his throat. Have a good one! Drive fast!

Until it's just us, resigned to one another.

One-way doors, everywhere. There is no turning back.

All I've ever known is apartments with, like, five roommates; other assholes like me. We would watch the bills change color, wait for the notice to appear tacked on the door. Then we'd cut out and leave the slumlord holding the bag.

We always moved in the middle of the night, fully hammered, never as sneaky as we thought we were. Imagine lots of crashing and thud-thud-thudding down the stairs, lots of laughing and shushing.

Now, it's apartments that don't belong to me. Where I've wound up after last call then stayed for days thereafter. I listen for a whispered conversation between roommates or a phone call in the other room: I don't know what to do. She just, won't, leave.

And then, onwards.

There's always that first impulse: I gotta tell you…

So I tell the Old Bastard, You've got the wrong books. These books are performance art. He offers me a line. A line of what?

Coke, Jesus, what kind of dirtbag do you think I am.

Exactly that kind of dirtbag.

Quit it, he says, or I'll get mad.

Dogs get mad, people get angry.

I've never had the money to get in deep with coke. What a riot, though. Whenever I do a line I'm a new person, and the first thing that new person wants is another line. Someone said that—not me, but someone.

The night limps on, sinuses packed with party powder, and my stories no longer take on a recognizable form. What will I come up with, I wonder, wanting to know.

I stub my toe hard, real hard, and am brought to my knees. In pain, I summon the truth: Fuck my fucking life, for real!

You sporked it good, the Old Bastard says, snickering. Hurts like hell, nothing you can do about it.

A life as a broken toe. A mind as a musty dusty warehouse: They're all in here, all the mistakes I've made. And yet—

I no longer watch my step. I fall with my arms by my side.

My shame spiral commences at the first sight of bright and early go-getters.

A Power Mom pushing a big-wheeled stroller, smiling, smiling.

A college student with a perfect ponytail, a yoga mat, a tote bag that says Spiritual Gangster.

A man in a suit outside a coffee shop, banging on the window, waving an employee over, pointing to his watch. What a dick.

Summertime, summertime of a bled-white sky. A hot breeze, then no breeze, a blistering set of circumstances compelling anything with a pulse to flee. Downtown, humans are replaced with the lumbering walking dead—chief among them, me, although I am barely here at all. My body thinks it is nighttime. I cannot trust my own senses. Heading in the direction of *away* is all I can do. Carrying on, from the fringe of the city to its beating heart and back again. Waiting out the clock. The library, I know, will open at noon.

I meet him around 3 p.m. I've met him every day for five days. He's seated at the bar, dead-eyed, with a glass of something neat and clear and mean-smelling.

He tosses me a cling-wrapped sandwich.

What's this?

Eat, he says. Old Crow's not meat.

So, no sleep for dinner tonight.

A drink appears before me. Who has been paying my way? I have. I pay with all of me.

Wait, no, let's modify that. I'm steeled with a kind of moxie that passes for pride. So maybe I come off as a good time gal. Maybe.

Blackout drunk has its appeal but I can't get there. A state once so familiar, now completely inaccessible. Like how I can't cry anymore. Something is alert within me. Who is it that's keeping the porch light on?

The company I keep demands disgrace and guilt, but only ever in hindsight. I once read that every cell in a human body will have turned over and been renewed within the course of seven years. Meaning, were I to live and breathe, there would come a time when the body I inhabit is a body untouched by him.

Which him? All the hims. Put them together, and what've you got? A smoldering garbage fire of unresolved mommy issues. Maybe a derivative punk band. Alcoholism too.

The world streams by me on the sidewalk and in the street. A hand emerges, grabbing for my shoulder. It's a moment before her face takes shape and registers.

How many blocks had she been following me, cutting through the crowd, calling out my name?

I haven't seen Suz for more than a year, not since she's had the baby, but here she is, unchanged in the ways that matter most. She wraps me in a hug, her arms holding on just a little bit tighter, just a little bit longer than mine.

How am I? What have I been up to? Where am I working these days?

I reach for my story—so well-honed and finely tuned. But there is nothing left. Only the truth remains. I hear the words uttered in my own voice. The first time I've said it out loud.

She reads the wounds lining my inner arms. Asks, Did you do this? and I nod. You'll stay with us, she says. Just like that.

A sober night on Suz's Goodwill couch, swaddled tight with acrylic throws, humidity be damned.

I sleep a dreamless sleep with my eyes squeezed shut.

AN ECONOMY OF PHRASING

That's how I can tell. *Server needed ASAP,* the ad says. *Ask for Jackie.* Necessity's sharp pinch: ASAP. They're hard up for help. I am too.

I've been here before, back when I was underage and fake ID'd. Rudy's: A damp and dark dive, without even a hint of irony. It reeks like the whole damn place is sticky to the touch.

A woman pores over the day's paper at the end of the bar by the kitchen doors. She's wiry and withered, with the look of a smoking habit that's finally caught up with her. A long cigarette pinched between her fingers. Like, No one's going to tell me I can't smoke in my own goddamn joint.

Jackie scans me from top to bottom, shaking her head. Her disdain, so pure it's practically clear. She lights another smoke, turns back to the obituaries without a word.

I tell her to take her time. I tell her I've got all day.

Fine, she snickers. Come back tonight at five and we'll see what you got.

I make a line toward the door to get ahead of any changes of heart. Jackie shouts out from behind me, bristling with the last word.

And wear something with sleeves, she says. For chrissakes, no one wants to see them Frankenstein arms of yours.

ॐ

I am the bungling shadow of another waitress, the only waitress—a keyed-up, smooth-faced marketing major named Melissa. She takes me through the do this, not that protocol; introduces me to the skeevy cooks whose names I won't commit to memory.

There's a tour of the walk-in and dry pantry, an overview of the menu. Mostly pub food—burgers, hot sandwiches, a grim selection of salads.

And brunch, a *bar* that serves brunch. A fresh hell in and of itself, the flames fanned with cheap cocktails and heavy-handed pours—this, according to Melissa. Her eyebrows stretch, her eyes widen: Do you know how many different ways people order eggs?

I nod, I smile, I laugh politely, all on cue. But I am the worst. I can't refill the water glasses without dumping ice all over the table. My lame jokes fall flat. And I'm so busy smiling and nodding that I'm not listening. I'm never listening.

Some guy, thirty-something with a thinning pompadour and an armful of pin-up tattoos. His is voice thick with Stoli, his hand pawing at my hip.

I know you, he says.

Yeah, well, it's Providence.

No, I mean … I saved you.

I hold his boozy glare.

You were wasted, he says. Outside Spock's. Maybe a month ago.

My face betrays nothing.

And some homeless-looking guy was all over you, trying to get you to leave with him …

Still, nothing.

Jesus, how 'bout a thank you or some—

I'm at work, man, and I turn on my heel.

He hooks my belt loop with his finger, pulls me toward him. My palm comes down on his wrist, hard. The sound of it, to me, like a gunshot fired underwater. My hand is hot and pulsing by my side. I feel nothing more as I slowly back away.

Welling in my chest, creeping up my throat, fanning across my eyes and my face. It's dread that I'm feeling. Thoughts and fears and fatal ways of being, rooting around in my mind, looking for a place to take hold. I step out into the side-alley. The door slams shut behind me, a gavel coming down.

The lit cigarette pinched between my fingers, I flip it upside down and bury it into my arm—a smoldering cherry, a searing brand, a perfect circle. I crumple with a ragged exhale, flick the butt. Peel myself off the pavement. I head back inside, back to work.

Jackie emerges from the back of the house. Melissa, screeching at the sight of her: Jackie, oh my god. Rosemary whacked a customer. Like, *literally*, she did. I couldn't believe it, I was like, oh my god, wait, did that just happen?

My heart jackhammers, but not in that old sought-after way. My heart beats too fast at the notion of something to lose.

Because he put his goddamn hands on me, is why. And I say it just like that, *goddamn hands.*

Jackie laughs. A sudden cackle, piqued with cruelty. Good for you, she wheezes. Cracks a beer, sets it before me with a wink. Turns out contempt for the customer is the name of the game at Rudy's, a policy that comes straight from the top.

I smile. I smile and it resonates within me as a kind of tenderness. Something I recognize but had forgotten about completely. I resist the urge to tamp it down. I give it a second.

Done for the day, another day, bellied up across from Jackie. She's scowling, left behind and tending bar until last call, until she's had it up to *here*—whichever comes first.

Jameson, I tell her, and throw down a ten. She snatches the bill as she pours. I go straight to the bottom of the glass and order another.

Looks like someone's tying it on tonight, Jackie says.

What's it to you, so long as I'm paying my own way.

She grumbles, grabs her Winstons, and moves toward the side-alley door, props it open with her hip. The late-summer sunset, a fan of golden light that reveals her in silhouette. Removed from the darkness of the bar she's smaller, delicate even, pulling on her cigarette like it's got the antidote.

I've never seen you step outside to smoke. It's weird. Like seeing a unicorn running down the street, or something.

My granddaughter's coming by tomorrow and I don't want it to reek in here.

I didn't know you were a grandma. I didn't even know you had a kid.

How would you, Jackie says, stamping out her smoke underfoot. You'd have to ask me about *me* to know something like that.

An absent moment twisting her hands, braiding a bar rag into her fingers. Her name's Ava, she says. The side door slams shut and jolts my response: Pretty.

Yeah, well. I don't get to see her a lot, she says.

I reach for something clever. Something to shut it down. Something about men or breakups or ungrateful kids. Nothing is there.

My daughter. … She drinks, Jackie says. She's been living with me since March, since the split.

The Patriots logo stretched across her flinty shoulders. A gentle *ting, ting, ting* as she wipes down the bottles and sets them back in place.

Y'know, I don't blame Abel for leaving, she says. My dad was a rummy—a real nasty drunk. So I know what that sort of thing does to a kid.

Me too.

Jackie spins around, sneering. Yeah, well. I don't need no pity, not from *you*, she says. Everyone's got problems.

Her weathered hands wringing a bar rag, her spindly frame buzzing with discomfort, her adamant gray gaze, her studied refusal to openly care—all of it, resisting the inertia of grief. I see her, the full picture of Jackie. How life is full of suffering, there's nothing special about it. That other people feel the way she feels. That everyone's got problems, yeah, but that doesn't make it hurt any less. That it's not her fault. These are things I could say to her, but don't.

She grabs the whiskey bottle by the neck. Tops me off, gives me the Knock. This round is on her. I shoot her an up-nod. Hold the full glass with both hands and go straight to the bottom.

A brain, making its best guess at what's out there in the world, and then providing a picture of it—a brain as a simulator. I am no steady state. Am I the *me* with the creeping dread, or the *me* who tamps it down; the *me* who feels some sort of way, or the *me* who acts some sort of way? And which *me* is the *me* that's always looking on?

I peel my eyes from the bar. Whatever it was I recognized is snuffed out. Like water to flame.

Suz appears before me in her kitchen. She says, We have to talk, with a measured tone that stops me in my tracks.

I ask if we can do this later, tell her I'm already late for work. But every fiber of my being makes a break for it as Suz says the words: You're going to have to find another place to stay.

Her mouth is making shapes, I see that, but nothing connects. From above, the kitchen looks like a scene from some movie I know by heart.

She's moving back in with her mom, her and the baby, but she doesn't want me to think I'm all alone again. She wants to help in anyway she can.

I hear my voice. It tells her not to worry. It says, I've been saving up, so I'll be okay. I haven't though. Not even a dollar.

I glance over her shoulder, inching towards the door.

Suz grabs my wrist, connects her eyes with mine. She says, This isn't your fault, Rosemary. I flinch at the sound of my name.

There's causation and there's condition. Logic links the two. My instinct keeps the differences known.

I move straight to the server's station, stash my bag underneath, and dig around for an apron.

Well, it's such an *honor* you decided to join us today, Melissa says. I keep my head down, put on a pot of regular and a pot of decaf. I roll the silverware.

Y'know you're almost a half hour late, she says, moving close beside me.

Nothing I can do about it now.

She points her acrylic fingertip in my face. I'm sick of your shit, she says. Sick, and, tired. Every shift, you show up late, hung over. Wearing the same friggin' clothes, what, like we wouldn't notice or anything.

Melissa keeps going with the pitch of a teakettle. It cuts deep. But her words mean nothing to my own ears. I hear them as a far off echo in a dead-black sea.

A party of four seats themselves in the farthest corner of the bar. IPA draft, rum and Diet, a Bloody and a Bud bottle, smile, nod, I'll be right back with those, and an even bigger smile. A nod and a thumbs-up for the couple at the two-top in the corner, air-writing for their check. Here we go, IPA draft, rum and Diet, a Bloody and a Bud bot—whoops, sorry, we'll just do a little switcheroo, IPA for you, Bud for you. Dread surges within me at the sound of *switcheroo*. In my chest and around my throat. Back over to the two-top couple in the corner with their bill. Drop the grenade, thanks so much, you guys have a great afternoon, and take cover before they can ask for anything else.

What I've got is probabilities—it is likely this will happen.

If this then that. If this then that.

Retribution. Punishment. There is no other way than this.

It's called karma, you idiot. Look it up.

Space opens up in the humidity around me, a chill that splinters the sweat down my arms, across my chest and my brow. It draws me back into my body. The *me* who feels some sort of way.

Then there's the gluey thwack of my footsteps behind the bar; my hand reaching for the green bottleneck, a clumsy pour nearly to the brim. I go straight to the bottom.

I step out for an hour between shifts. *Less* than an hour. Just long enough to take a breather, to get a real cup of coffee and a fresh pack of cigarettes.

Melissa's behind the bar when I return, bubbling with some sort of something. She's gloating. Jackie wants to talk to you in her office, she says. Right away.

Everything rolls out thick as glue. Passing through the swinging double doors. Through the kitchen. Past the walk-in where the skeevy cooks are smoking weed.

Jackie's office door is open.

The darkness of the room, the glow of the computer screen playing on her face, smoke circling her head and neck, all for emphasis.

She holds up her hand, stops me at the threshold. You want to tell me why you think you can steal from me?

Kettledrums boom.

Melissa told me she's seen you sneaking whiskey this morning during brunch.

Kettledrums boom louder. She isn't wrong.

You think I wouldn't find out? Y'know, with all your bullshit I put up with, and this is how you treat me? Like I'm some kind of idiot doormat?

Words build in my throat: a confession exceeding circumstance, a punishing desperation that wants to be seen.

My instinct redoubles instead.

I sneer and it shakes off the dread of everything and nothing. I laugh in her face and it's a choice that can't be un-chosen. I pull some cash from my pocket. A twenty, crumpled into a ball and tossed onto her desk.

There—that ought to cover it.

Get out of here. Get the fuck out of my office now. You're fired.

A snicker and another laugh. I got to hand it to you, Jackie. It's impressive. You're *the* most malignant cunt I've ever met.

Her congested scream.

The stoned cooks. Their barely-contained laughter.

The kitchen.

The swinging double doors.

Melissa cutting limes at the bar. She looks up without eye contact.

My voice is a low and slow growl, determined to hurt. I tell her sleeping around and snorting Adderall aren't skills she can include on her résumé. That she'll learn the hard way when she finally moves out of her parents' house, when she finally finishes her shitty Associates Degree. I tell her she's a fucking idiot. That she's got no one to blame but herself.

My voice keeps going until Melissa's eyes blink with pain.

I huddle up in a seat towards the back of the bus. Outside there's a sweep of darkness, a cloud passing over the sun, and my reflection appears in the window. This distant curiosity: a face paled to skim-milk blue, a body like a bag of wire hangers. The sun reemerges. The sky brightens and I am nowhere.

I take the 16 all the way to Galilee, to the Salty Brine Beach. A measly sand patch alongside the Block Island ferry launch. There's a small group gathered, cackling and hoarse, speaking a musical blend of Portuguese and English. The beer in a can set, the white wine with ice in a thermos set. Older looking, but younger than they look. They've been at it all day.

The tide shrugs around my hips, some lapping diesel rainbow. A voice shouts: Take the plunge, hon! Once your crotch is in you can't feel the cold water no more! The voice, a woman on the sand, waving, clapping, laughing, coaxing me on. Her t-shirt says, *Someone Cares. I Don't, But Someone Does.*

Ears back, belly up, arms stretched out open wide, a body drawn out to sea. The ferry motors into Narragansett Bay and rips the tide to the left. The rainbow water takes you.

That thing you did as a kid, squinting, smushing something in the distance with your thumb and forefinger. You smush the setting sun, a delivery truck, the ferry chugging towards the horizon. You smush the EMTs running towards the water, towards you. Purposeful strides in purposeful blue uniforms.

I SENSE IT BEFORE I FEEL IT

I feel it before I hear it; hear it before I recognize what it is. The gaining volume of fluorescent lights overhead. Freshly laundered linens piled neatly at the foot of the bed across the room. They say, You're alone in here but not for long.

She enters on the balls of her feet, already outfitted in the papery johnnie and treaded socks get-up. Her folded street clothes held to her chest like textbooks. Round face, dark downturned eyes—she's melancholic and angelic, a painting of a martyred saint. Seems cruel, exposing someone like her to this place. Like she might catch it or something. Like it's airborne. Claudia introduces herself. I respond with unyielding silence.

A drop-ceiling above. Broken acoustic tiles, once white, now covered with water stains. The dingy pastiche, a work of art. Cypresses reaching for heaven. Sweeping brushstrokes and glimpses of sky, despairing irises and heavy-headed sunflowers. A divine pastoral, a day at the park, a view of a better world.

Claudia jolts upright at the sight of her, the small woman hesitating in the doorway. Tote bags dangling from the crook of each elbow, overloaded with the comforts of home. Her distress unhidden; eyes red-rimmed and misty but unmistakably dark and downturned. The small woman plunges into the room, arms outstretched. Wraps her daughter in a full embrace.

Fuck this shit, I say, and snap the covers over me. I roll onto my side and face the barred window. The fluorescent lights thrum overhead.

The social worker asks me how I got here, but *wound up here* is what he means. I shrug.

Well, how are you feeling?

I cannot tear out a single page of my life, I tell him, *but I can throw the whole book in the fire*.

He asks if I'm a poet, and I say no, I'm just a Pisces. He nods, unamused, and jots in the open file on his lap. The line is obscure, and that is the point. I am using all that I've read for screening purposes.

The social worker reaches into the business-looking bag by his chair and produces a bunch of tiny papers. I flinch at the sight of them. Sticky notes, all of them stuck together. These were found in your backpack, he says, placing the pile before me. And he waits, blinking, because he has been trained to let me do the explaining.

One note says *Space Rendezvous, Lunar Acrobat, Every Day is Summer in Space*, all in box lettering. Band names. I had wanted to form a band so I could name a band. People have babies just to name humans, is how I saw it. Another note is more of the same. *These Days: This is our daughter Ellipses / And our son Hat / And that's our dog Katherine*.

Something I stand behind—*Hemingway was a dilettante*. I'd even circled it for emphasis.

The exile dreams of a glorious return: a relict of a day spent bellied up at Spock's, talking to anyone who'd listen. I'd fallen down hard and the bartender bounced me. I didn't have any money to pay up, not even a dime, and the bartender threatened to call the cops. I begged him: Do it. Please, do it.

And then there's one that's a furious scrawl. It says *diseased memory* over and over.

The social worker points to one note in particular. He says it stands out among the rest. *A pig is no longer a pig when it's a dead pig.* What does it mean, he wants to know, as if it means anything more than what it says.

I thought all you people would be home right now, shutting the fuck up. Intrusive thoughts, still-frames and sounds and smells—a bus ride as a hellscape.

Don't let the wish be the mother of the thought.

A party I heard through the wall, a party I came to leave.

Ice to water, water to vapor, I am gone.

And then I was admitted. There's no note for that.

A nurse had been assigned to watch me shower and use the bathroom. A nice enough nurse with a worn-through smile.

I ask the social worker what happened. He says she lost her job. All of them on the ward, in the hospital, they had to rethink their protocols in light of the incident.

It's a shame that weary nurse was fired—that weary nurse saved my life.

The social worker puts down his pen and eyeballs me intently. Do I understand my role in the nurse's termination? My doing, my tying and knotting, my adaptability to the impossible—what's meant to be impossible on this ward, by design?

Render the objects. Render the characters through observation.

A white tab for sleep. Sleep as a weighted feeling. Waking is not waking. It's a gentle poke in the side. A silent line of us, all of us lined up at dawn. The kinetic doings of the nurses' station, the squeeze of a blood pressure cuff, paper cups of pills and paper cups of apple juice.

And this poor guy. He logged an adult lifetime of working hard for his family and ran himself ragged. He went ahead and blew a gasket. Now his days are spent pacing—nights too. Together we watch reruns of *Walker Texas Ranger* before breakfast. Me and him and Chuck Norris delighting in wrongs made right.

Everywhere, there is the subliminal fragrance of inevitability, here on the Incurable Ward. Which means it's my fault for failing to prepare.

My mother had visited when I was here the first time. She arrived with boxes of donuts, enough for the whole staff. Make sure the doctors get some too, she'd said loudly. When it was just the two of us, visiting alone behind an unlocked door, she didn't ask how I was feeling. My mother wanted to know, What are you *telling* them?

Typical summertime fare: Overcooked pot roast served without a knife. Here time is stopped cold.

I don't recognize him, but the food service guy recognizes me. From the bar, he whispers. You know, you're not the only one from Spock's I've seen come through here.

And this information is meant to do … what?

There is a world of gossip happening on the outside, in and around my old haunts. I'm sure of it. Because when that Old Bastard hit me, I hit him back—harder. He must've worn the shiner for a week.

That's me doing my part, like how I've always said some men would do well with a punch in the face. I'm doing all I can for the community.

Moving in the direction of greater and greater abstraction is the only way. So, from here on out…

I am not quite myself, I think. Or am I my most self? Here—with the scrim scraped away. Cracked wide open for all to see. It's a brave new world. And it's exhausting.

We are counted, recorded, thrown together, and cast aside. Their assessments are nothing we did not already know.

Some people in the Group like to drum up a hard luck story. Some of us keep it under wraps. These dramas are repetitive and hopeless but not without a laugh.

Words have meaning, it's true. But certain words are used incorrectly so often that they've been leeched of their meaning entirely. So when I tell her, I *literally* couldn't care less about you, I'm concerned she doesn't believe me. And this Lisa, she stands up so suddenly her chair falls back. She storms off screaming, I'm moving to space 'cause yous don't know how to treat each other!

Am I a crybaby, or am I a bully? Or do you not know what the hell you're talking about?

Seems my diagnosis is contingent. They're revising. When they tell me what's wrong with me it sounds like a condemnation. Like there's morality attached. What's worse is, the Madonna song of the same name is stuck in my head now.

The doctor brushes me off. He says a defective question is a question that sounds like a question but really isn't. For instance—why?

I hate him in ways that are almost rejuvenating.

The words *elopement risk* are spelled out on my door. Not on a sticky note, on a paperboard sign that's tacked up with care.

They won't let me have a pen and there's nothing here to read. The ceiling is higher than I remember—the pale green walls have been painted a dusky blue since last time. Voices pervade the hallway, echoing in a round like "Row, Row, Row Your Boat."

The social worker won't quit. Still, he tries for a connecting moment.

What is your happiest memory? he asks.

My what?

Happiest memory.

What.

I am incredulous, though I've heard him perfectly well. I want to be sure *he* hears him.

My mother wanted me held that first time. For as long as it takes, she'd said.

She saw my future as a white room with rows of white beds. She saw nurses as babysitters and orderlies as cops. The doctor, then, was at a loss. I don't think you understand the situation, he'd said. Which was a nice way of saying my mother had seen too many movies.

You shall know the tree by the fruit it bears, motherfuckers.

My family's greatest hits include:

Everyone's got problems, what makes you think you're so special?

What happens in this house stays in this house.

Stop crying—no one's listening and no one cares.

There are people who get day passes. Not me, but some people. Family members appear on the ward. They sign-out their loved ones and promise to have them back by supper. Their promises mean something.

A day pass is a goal to work toward, the social worker says. Except no one is coming for me. I've no one to sign me out, take me around, suggest a world outside these walls and outside myself that makes life worth living.

A new patient arrived yesterday. A boy grown old in the body of a man—a mountain. The staff take turns pacing alongside him. Up and back at a gentle clip, up and back. He sings all day long. The melody changes but the refrain stays the same.

When he gets upset security is called. Six men arrive wearing black rubber gloves. They subdue him with arms and elbows. It changes his tune. His sweet boy words with the timbre of a grown man: I hurt! he says. You hurt me!

His words are his. They cut to the quick.

We just want you safe, is what the weary nurse had told me.

AUTUMN

IF THIS THEN THAT

A cold snap, the intrusion of cause and effect as sunlight dims and temps drop. An enormous string of causal events.

I had held onto their house key as a card to play when the time was right. They head out of town for Columbus Day weekend and the whole week thereafter. They always do, come hell or high water. I've been counting on it all along.

The key turns over between my fingertips; the deadbolt retreats. I step into the dark relief of their living room, crumple into the couch. My eyelids made heavy by the aroma of fresh laundry, perfumed cleansers, warming spices.

I sense my parents before I see them—my pulse booming. My scars, my purple seams, aching in time. The slam of their car door, a mortar blast that rings throughout the grid of tract houses. My mother glares at me through the front door window, fumbling with her keys, clumsy with rage.

I leave without a fight. There's no fight left in me as they cast me out once more. I am hollow, but I am heavier than when I arrived days before. Weighted with three rolls of quarters I found in a desk drawer, two sweaters, a pair of sneakers, two bottles of shitty wine.

ℒ

I awake in a motel. In a motel, I can be anyone. I rifle through the drawers looking for—what?

I go out to find someone. Anyone. A bike messenger I've seen around does the trick. Smelly, sinewy, and tan with a dog-bite haircut. He checks-in his fixed-gear at the front desk, flirts with the night clerk. He asks who's footing the bill, and I—

I no longer remember that things have ever been any other way.

An abundance of dooming cosmos, but not out of nowhere. Lunar eclipse in my house of dysphoric mood states.

What I need is a psychic. I'm interested in the why of it all, those peculiar idiosyncrasies as inherent to my nature as drawing breath. Like—why does ketchup make me gag? Why do I get panicky swimming in fresh water? Why am I undone by the sound of a vacuum cleaner?

Specifically, why am I like this?

These ways of being, plugged into something beyond me.

But, really? The why is simple. It's the reason that eludes me.

Humans have been doing this ever since we began to notice. We can't help it. We are the organism that wants to *know*.

Just when I think nothing could possibly surprise me, not anymore, not after everything, I see a driver toss a greasy, overstuffed McDonald's bag out the window of their moving vehicle. Littering! And I—I just, can't, believe it.

A church downtown promoting their Traditional Latin Mass, like inaccessibility is the point. Which makes me think, that is where I need to be. Tell me, for the love of god. Tell me what's wrong with me.

You, the one in the getup: I trust that I could convince myself to trust you. Just tell me you have the answers, please. Or tell me I'm wrong. That it's all my fault, that there's power in admitting I alone am to blame. Because if I am living a choice I can simply un-choose, then I will just un-choose it. I will get on with the damn thing, or I will throw in the towel once and for all.

Plato called it *katharsis*. Purification is what he was getting at. Release.

But whoever it is, circling through downtown in an old Buick, blasting the *Halloween* theme music, they understand everything.

The Jesus people. There is always a group of them handing out pamphlets in Kennedy Plaza. They ignore me now. I don't know—I guess I kind of take it personally. They recognized the risen Christ by his wounds. I ought to open up my arms again, this time just for them. Like—see? I just might be.

My secret self is the one who talks to god, begging for help. Altogether, a most unlikely event.

I have found a broken watch. The broken watch I've found is not an omen. The universe doesn't have a cerebral cortex. So *omen* is merely a noun that doesn't do justice to the reality I am trying to explain.

And yet—

I can't shake this sense of urgency. The sense of urgency is unshakable because the urgency is fucking real. The seasons are clicking, as seasons do.

Flinty, is what November smells like.

Smells like imminent frost.

His youth grabs my attention. The kid is a *kid*.

See that car over there? That guy? the kid says.

That guy in that car will pay me forty bucks for services I am not offering or advertising. This, according to the kid.

D'you hear me? That's a lot of money—you saying no, for real?

The only words I can manage: Where is your mother?

The kid flinches, turns on his heel, and runs back to the faceless driver.

A depth of sound surges through the liquor store parking lot. The car door opening with a peal, slamming like a trap being sprung. Heavy footfalls that move toward me, crackling gravel beneath each step. Twenty paces, I figure, maybe less.

My heartbeat fills the full space of my ribcage. Not as a sound, as a sensation. I squeeze my eyes shut, resisting the moment within and without.

A girl's memory—the man-sized silhouette that filled her doorway, the boots that staggered across her bedroom floor.

Footsteps cease beside me. The cold air keeps his smell all around him—a damp cloud of clear liquor. No one could tell his breath takes my breath away.

Don't make me put you in that car.

My face betrays nothing. It meets his faceless face. I answer in a voice that says fuck you very much, do your worst.

His hand wraps around the whole of my forearm, fingers to thumb with a full grip. His hand squeezes, lifts, yanks.

A bolt fires through me. I reach for my self and yank back. Stand upright with a start. Bury my knee into his softest parts. Force the butt of my hand into his nose as he folds in half.

It's how my father taught me to defend myself, with lessons learned the hard way.

WINTER

SLOW AT FIRST

Then faster and faster for warmth. A glimpse of a moment in midair, and I land in a pile at the curb.

A car passes by and slows to a crawl. I hear it through the closed windows, through the heavy bass of the stereo—the distinct pitch of laughter, young women laughing as one.

I wrestle with the black ice, get a grip, get my feet back under me. The bus stop, a frozen bench that stings through the seat of my jeans. I rub my knee, mumbling, cursing the pain that will fill it tomorrow.

My jacket is no match for the bracing cold. I lifted it from Spock's a few nights ago, where the art students come out in droves. I slipped in just before last call when the place was wasted and oblivious, careening through '80s pop tunes.

I warm the coins in my pocket with the heat of my hand. If I warm them, will they warm me? Two dimes rubbed together?

He sits beside me but lets me be. A bundled-up man, fifty-ish, a face clouded with sad bastard stories and rot-gut liquor. His lit cigarette dances between his lips, lips dancing with cold.

Can I get one of those?

He flinches at the sound of my voice. Sure thing, Freckles. He fumbles in his pocket, pinches one between his thumb and index finger. A half-smoked butt offered like a single flower. People ever call you Freckles?

Never twice, they don't.

He laughs a roaring laugh that becomes a gluey cough, doubling him over. His smoke drops and rolls across the sidewalk. He snatches it up from the gutter and resets it at the corner of his mouth. Still wheezing, he scrabbles to get his plastic lighter going, sparking and mostly spent. Y'know these things'll kill you.

I look into the tiny flame jittering under my nose and take a long pull. Tell him that's the idea.

Ernie introduces himself. I draw another drag and speak my name through the smoke.

A cigarette to keep breathing, a means to draw breath. I think—oh, how I think—so I can confirm, yes, I am here.

It's a solution suited to circumstance: the chance of an invite to wherever he's headed. Looking down the barrel of nighttime, there's no other remedy. Every night is one night closer to the longest night of the year.

Considerations for living in a body on the street: What if I don't pay my way with all of me? I notice the creak in my chest with quiet fascination, the slam of doors opening and closing. Some would call it instinct, but I wouldn't. My instincts don't have my best interest at heart.

The bus's LED sign appears high above the stream of headlights. Don't tell me this is where we part ways.

I say, I don't have any cash on me so I'll be walking—it isn't untrue.

Ernie's hand disappears deep into his pocket and produces a bus pass, a punch ticket held up high like the final reveal of a magic trick.

Can't leave a pretty girl to walk in the cold, he says.

He talks like he hasn't talked in days—not to a person. A guy like him, a *let me tell ya something* sort of guy—you cut them slack, or you shut them up. He talks and talks, and I let him.

His eyes say he's run hard, that he's gone to the bottom of a bottle. But his face bears traces of a life before—rows of smile lines that reveal the full range of his humanity. My face is a black hole, a vacuuming energy that reveals nothing. Who should be afraid of whom?

The heat on the bus is fully cranked. I take off my jacket for the first time in who knows how long. I am out of the cold, thanks to Ernie, and tell him so.

His gaze changes. It peers beneath the appearance of things. He blows a raspberry, shakes his head, an over-the-top show.

I tell ya, kid, you gotta get up early in the morning to surprise 'ol Ernie. Damn, if you ain't surprising me.

I've got that going for me, I guess.

How you holding up? It's tits cold out there, getting colder.

One foot in front of the other.

You got a habit or something?

Or something. And something continues. Something grows. I have no idea what I'm doing. I'm mostly sad and tired and sad, aren't you?

And Ernie winces. He looks away.

There's a church down Newport, he says. The charitable kind. They do what they can at Christmastime. He fesses up. He's hoping for help too.

My heartbeat fills all of me. I feel it and I feel maybe I have a chance.

So—I will sing for my supper. I will wait in line. There are many before me and behind me; some have brought their kids along. One at a time we enter a musty room. Not in the church, but adjacent.

The idea is this: You state your case. Hat in hand, you share your tale of woe.

They're seated at a table, all of them on the same side facing out. One has a large bound checkbook, a pen in hand.

I stand before them and feel their gaze. These three old women, permed and blue-haired, buttoned up and measuring. I consider myself as they might see me, if I look to them worthy of care and concern. I've kept my hair neat; my face is paled to translucence but unblemished and clear. The obviousness of my intention stabs at me. Pangs of shame and anger and grief. What am I trying to say without saying a word? It's not about where I am, it's about where these women think I belong. That, or someone should just kill me before the damage spreads because I have no one to blame but myself.

I tell them I don't know what to say, and I mean it.

Well, tell us what's brought you here, says the one in the middle, the one with the checkbook.

You start where you are. Or where you *were*.

No, I don't have anyone, I answer. No, I don't have a home to return to.

I push up my sleeve, revealing my tale of woe: a deeply livid bruise, the exact size and shape of a man's hand, wrapping my forearm. It's deadly out there, I tell them.

And what about the ... the *other* one there? My seam, a revenant of thirty-six stitches. Months later and still it gleams violet from wrist to elbow.

Do I consider it a sin? I'm not sure, I say, but I've lived to tell the tale and that counts for something, right? As if a bad answer is better than no answer.

They believe me—the three old ladies. The check they write suggests they do.

Because there's a storm coming, one says.

A Nor'easter, another adds. Could get up to a foot and a half.

Because it's Christmastime, they say all together.

My *thank you* emerges as a voice unbroken. A bell ringing.

I didn't ask and he didn't offer, but still Ernie leads the way. He keeps his head down, shoulders rounded to guard against the wind, gathering stamped-out cigarettes from the ground, anything with a few drags left to the filter. He finds a quarter. Holds it up with a smile.

The walk is long and cold—winding from the Newport of touristy delights, shops and pubs and seafood joints; beyond the lived-in grids of raised ranches and row houses; past the strip-malls and supermarkets.

I think about check-in and the thinking makes me antsy. Me with only my word to go on. Those three old birds knew the score. The check isn't written out to me, or written out to cash. It's payable to the Pineapple Inn—they even knew the cost of a two-week stay.

I'll just wait out here, Ernie says, and I see that he left the church empty-handed. That something about his story was found to be lacking. That, according to those women and all that they stand for, Ernie was living a choice he could simply un-choose. Ernie would wait. For me.

An electronic ding. A woman behind the desk. She looks up with a smile. I draw the folded check from my pocket and will my hand steady. Her smile falls away. She calls out and a man fills the doorway behind the desk. Fuzzy brows knit together, chin lowered, chest inflated beneath his sweater. This angry man, the angry owner.

He comes from around the desk, plucks the check from my hand, and squares himself akimbo. Studies the check, my face, then all of me from head to toe. They give you two weeks, he says. They must believe you good.

The owner looks to the young woman and shoots her an up-nod. She retrieves a key, hands it over. Whatever it is he whispers to her is all rolling tongue and hard k's.

That guy out there, he your friend? the owner asks, all in his throat. It resonates off the tile floor and within me.

I read the room: He's not my friend. He showed me the way, is all, only because the bus doesn't run here on the weekend. But we're not *friends*.

My spat-out emphasis makes my stomach churn.

I give you room where I see you, he says, pointing out the window to a peeling yellow door across the parking lot. If I see that rat, he adds, you go. I don't care about church ladies.

Eyes averted—meek and nodding. I am a girl scolded but spared the rod.

A caricature of a Shitty Motel Room. Diffused light the color of dishwater, dirt-cheap carpet and bedspread, an imbrication of invisible human grime. Stale air made thicker with stale smoke. A TV I'd put to good use.

I cross the threshold with Ernie on my heels. I turn to face him and notice for the first time his tiny frame. I claim the five inches I have on him. Summon all of my shittiness, all of my selfishness.

My apology is thin.

Ernie's eyes beg the question. He says nothing. He shuffles from one foot to the other, fidgeting with the too-big shoulders of his jacket. Tamping it down, whatever it is, clanging around in his mind looking for a way to sound off. Some sort of feeling linked to a memory linked to a feeling. He draws all of himself onto the balls of his feet and meets my eyes, holding the half-smoked cigarettes before him. An offering.

My chin falls to my chest. I shake my head no.

The owner glares at us through the office window across the parking lot. I feel his disgust, as deep down as I can feel. He's all venom, even as Ernie turns to make his way back to somewhere else.

I sit on the bed because there's nowhere else to sit. I drink black coffee—instant, only as hot as the faucet will go.

When the owner knocks, he knocks like a cop. I open the door and he pushes by me without a word. He marches into the bathroom. He draws back the shower curtain. He looks everywhere there is to look in this room where there are not many places to look. It's quiet as a grave when his stomping feet are gone.

The coffee keeps me company. My heart kicks; the tender parts of my arms quiver. I am in my body. But I am not alone.

In my dream we're arsonists. For a handsome fee, me and Ernie will burn your place to the ground.

Here's the thing: We use rats. Dip them whole into lighter fluid and turn them loose. We give it some time, the rats grubbing around in the walls and crawl spaces, under the floorboards.

The building goes up with a single match thrown. We both delight in the blaze. So hot and bright, we take off our jackets and sweaters, our socks and our shoes.

All the while, I hear those rats.

PEOPLE DON'T CHANGE

Not unless they've lost something important, something that cannot be regained. And even then—

The bus driver doesn't say a word; he just lets me ride. So I ride for hours, dragging out the task at hand. I'm saying goodbye to these great heights. They've kept me going on the sidewalk and in the streets. Soon, we'll be parting ways.

Squealing brakes, a shuddering stop, and the driver announces to only me that his shift is through. I step from the bus to the sidewalk without a word.

I am headed to the place I was supposed to go back when I got out. Accepting the truth over what I wish the truth was, and other things that had previously seemed impossible.

I tell the woman behind the glass, I'm a little late for my appointment. How late is late? she asks, because she is a person with a job and a plan who believes in the meaning of time.

Seated before another bearded motherfucker. He's got my hair shirt all laid out and waiting for me.

I see you were discharged two months ago. Why didn't you keep your follow-up appointment for aftercare?

The doctor asks this as if the answer is not abundantly clear. As if I am not a person erased, afraid to stand still. My mind, both cause and effect—two sides of one fact. Mania, but in the way it is often used colloquially, the head's name for the heart's excesses.

No, more like a well-worn groove, a voice ruminating with clicks and buzzes. Notice me, it says. Or I'll kick in the fucking door.

Here I am limited to consequences. Consequences are *it*. I'm acting in ways I don't understand, I tell him. Even the parts of me that want me dead think they have my best interest at heart.

Pressured speech, racing thoughts—any case I make is arbitrary. But the bearded brain doc can't get over my days spent reading, trying to read, rereading the same sentence.

That's interesting, he says. That you ... that you're able to ... I mean, most people, in the state you're in, they're not—

Not what? What am I supposed to do? Tell me—what would you have me do? *In the state I'm in?*

His look of surprise is not a delighted one.

Maybe I'm just more trouble than I'm worth.

Well, you certainly are trouble, he says.

I leave the mental health clinic with three paper scripts. There's not much else I can do for you, he says, handing them off. You can get these filled downstairs, no charge. Beyond that ...

And he shrugs. Shrugs!

It's a real problem, this living in the world. Call it a soft suicide.

The year is through. I am tired of getting by.

SPRING

HALF IN HALF OUT

I want to linger in twilight sleep. Where I no longer require convincing, where I'm capable of wanting more than what I've come to expect.

Instead, I'm met with the coarse feel of industrial sheets against my cheek. The plastic rustle of a mattress cover. My torso dipping awkwardly into the crimped contour beneath me. My lashes pry apart. My eyes adjust. I'm in my body, in my cot. I fold it up every morning. Unfold it every night.

I have slept in the shelter for sixty-one nights.

Forty-two in the *shelter* shelter where I was signed-in every night at five, kicked out every morning at eight. It demanded punctuality. Nothing was guaranteed, no matter how long I had been sleeping there. Six bunks for twelve women, never more, never less.

Now I sleep in a room with a door that locks, a room I share with Deb.

The shelter director, Betty, she'd pulled me aside and told me a bed had become available in one of the doubles. She thought that bed should go to me. The rest of the staff had agreed. I was cutting the line, Betty said. There were other women who'd been at the shelter longer. Did I want to share a double with Deb? As if I'd say no.

It's not big, our room. Two cots with a night stand in between. A small kitchenette with a fridge. Our own bathroom. The shower head is missing but the pressure is ferocious and more than makes up for it. My first night in there, I stood under the hot water until I was purple and lightheaded.

Each of us has a particleboard armoire. I hang everything up when it's not on my body. It makes me feel something, seeing my stuff in there.

There was this woman Katie who had stayed at the shelter for months—a *young* woman, younger than me. Katie ran around for three weeks telling anyone who'd listen that she was pregnant, except she wasn't. Deb narced when she found out. She said Katie was like a daughter to her, that she felt betrayed by her lies. So she told and told and told.

Katie wanted someone to treat her with care, even if it meant inhabiting a fiction. That's how I saw it. But Katie broke the rules—something about liability. She was booted from the shelter, barred from ever returning.

My bed had been hers.

Days pass with a million zips of a razor, countless cruxes of cardboard under foot. I'm glad for it. I can do anything, it seems, as long as I do it every day.

Me and Linda lift and count and break down boxes. She's my mother's age, with twin sons my age. Both live at home. She's happy to have 'em, Linda says often. Her Boys. That's what she calls them, husband included. She smiles when she says it.

We're not the only ones who work back in the stockroom, just the only ones who talk while we're at it. She talks. I nod. Linda's got a lapping rhythm. Can I believe she's in her fifties? Hauling inventory keeps her in fighting form, she says. She has to have strong arms to ride her Harley. Did she tell me about her Harley? Her Boys ride too. They head up to Laconia for Bike Week every year. It's something they do together.

I'm cued up from time to time. Linda pauses, her eyebrows stretched in anticipation. I hit my mark: You're *right*, I tell her, and she laughs. Throws her hands up in a show of motherly martyrdom, I *know*, right? She goes and goes and spares me from having to talk about myself. Why I wear the same clothes every day, why I smoke through lunch. She spares me from talking about where I live, assuming I have a place here in Providence—with all the other *arty* kids, she says. I never correct her.

My timing couldn't have been worse, looking for a job back in January. Service staff gets carved to the bone after the Holidays. I knew as much but had no choice. I rolled the dice, headed to the mall up Providence. Filled out fifteen applications in a single day. Start date? *ASAP*. Wage requested? *Negotiable*. Availability? *Sunday through Saturday, open to close.*

From store to store, I had insisted on speaking with the hiring manager. Handed them my application with a smile.

I passed. It worked.

Now I long for the ordinary. Khaki pants and coupon clipping, cell phone plans, extra sugary coffee, diet tips, and reality TV. It's better than being at large. Daily bread and monotony have taken on the look of a miracle.

I had been hard up when I walked through the shelter door. What, with the meds drawing me back in my body and my time at the Pineapple Inn ending unceremoniously on New Year's Day.

Betty led me into the office, poured me a cup of coffee. Told me a bit about the place. The McKinney Shelter in Newport—one mile, one million light years away from the hedge-rowed mansions of Bellevue Avenue and the Tennis Hall of Fame.

She offered me a bus pass. Suggested I head over to Human Services, sign up for food stamps and state assistance. I declined, told her that sort of thing is for people who are really in need. Her brow furrowed. She said nothing.

I just need a job, I told her. A job and a place to stay.

Betty sat upright, squared her body in my direction. What are you doing here, Rosemary?

An absent moment, I swallowed hard.

I was hospitalized, I said. A few times. And everything just ... fell apart. Which wasn't the whole story.

And your family? I shook my head no. Which was the whole story. I told her it's okay. I'm okay now. They put me on new meds, the right meds. I take them every day. Quit drinking too. This has all been my fault, I said. Some lessons can only be learned the hard way.

I told her I'd think about it—the food stamps, that is. But I took the bus pass and thanked her.

That night I slept with my shoes on, unwilling to soften. Clutched my backpack close, my greasy, bulging backpack as a little spoon, and kept my coat buttoned to the collar. The only bed available was a top bunk alongside a drafty window, rattling leaded glass above Marlborough Street. The bitter cold swept up from the Bay, crept through all of me, and gave the night a strange austerity. Not safety, no, but shelter.

I am never far from my nook. I see it when I get off the bus in the morning. It's a ten-minute walk from the mall where I work. The nights I spent under those stairs intrude on my memory from time to time. How I sang every song I knew just to stay awake.

But it's a good thing. I see my nook and I act accordingly. I do what I can. I have divested myself from myself. I feel a lot of things. Feelings aren't facts. Here is what I know for sure: I am safe so long as I am on guard, even when I am safe. It requires I keep one foot in front of the other. Forward, always.

There are no answers for me in all that has passed. Sifting through the why's and the how's and the what if's—it's like drinking milk when I am thirsty for water.

Why does the water taste like milk?

I'm good at not thinking about them. I've had a lot of practice—it's been almost a year. What helps is, I think they were right, when they said I'm beyond repair. My mother delivered her parting shot at the top of her lungs through her front door. She said, You should be grateful I still care about you despite knowing what you really are.

What, not who.

An effective jab is one you suspect to be true.

Some cologne-drenched shoe salesman pops his head in the stockroom. Girls hauling stock, he says, laughing. Had to see it for myself. Guess Filene's is hip to the feminist agenda. Good on you two—give 'em hell!

Linda's face turns stormy and clenched. Not me, nuh uh, no way. The world is what you make of it, she says, and I ain't no one's victim. She turns to me for reinforcement, for my know-nothing response: You're *right*, I say.

Linda is also, as far as I can tell, a climate change denier and, in that way, ought to be excused from jury selection. Facts? Evidence? For what? But I am toothless at work. I'd like to get it done, thank you, I'd like to get on with it.

I *know*, right?

Is there a good way to learn you have holes in your sneakers? In March? No—no, there is not.

What I should do is, I should cut down a few squares of cardboard, just fashion myself some insoles. I think of all my *shoulds* at a time like this. If I were smart, I'd remember what I'm saving for.

My wish for a knowable home is a thought. The thought, a well-worn groove of my memory. Two weeks on the futon in my parent's basement after I was discharged last March. Two weeks before my mother grew offended by my wallowing, incensed by my excuses, my unwillingness to snap out of it. Two weeks before she reached her limit. She had all she could stand and no she didn't care really because it wasn't even her idea in the first place. It was that pushy doctor who'd insisted—the know-it-all social worker too. You must've really snowed those quacks over with your sob stories, she had said, but that wasn't gonna work on her.

Wait, *no*. No, no, no. My safety relies on lessening, lightening to survive.

I have cast out retentive memory. I shall have no more of thee!

Two employees chat at the cash wrap, decked out in their referee-striped uniforms. They greet me with vigor, but turn cold as I head for the sales rack.

A pair of Chucks stop me dead. Shiny, shiny black. Fake patent leather.

Do you have these in a ten, I ask, holding the sneaker up high. They answer with matching shrugs. Well, can you check please? Matching eye rolls. One heads into the back, returns empty-handed.

Maybe a nine-and-a-half?

No half sizes, they say.

I guess a nine, then.

I lace them up quick, glance at the angled mirror by my feet.

I'd like to wear them out, if that's okay.

I toss my holey shoes as I dash for the bus. Cast off, they look woeful—all salt-stained and gray, poised atop the overflowing trashcan.

The bus is in sight, parked with the engine running. Passengers are lining up, and my long strides become a trot. Two blocks away, two minutes before it departs, and my trot becomes an all-out sprint.

The plastic edges are razors against my Achilles tendons. The pounding pavement tamps my toes into a hoof. I roll my body weight to the outer edge of each foot to shift the pressure, to shift something. Steady my breath to withstand the brunt of it, like biting down on a leather strap.

They'd break in, probably. I'd get used to them, these too-small shoes. They're plastic and agonizing, but they're shiny and new. I cannot take them off. I'll never get them back on.

Aspiration means looking forward, it means drawing breath. My bane and my antidote are before me, fogging up the bus window.

I get by the shelter office unnoticed. Betty's in there wrangling some old guy I recognize. She's turning him away because he's fall-down wasted, but this old guy isn't having it. He'll keep Betty busy for a while, at least until the ambulance shows up.

I take the elevator up a single floor. The doors part and reveal a smiling Deb.

I got one for you, she says, dancing from foot to foot. Why can't dinosaurs clap their hands?

Why?

'Cause they're dead!

That's a good one, Deb.

She looms behind me as I fuss with the sticky lock.

Just so y'know, I'm sleeping up in Joey's room tonight, she says. Our little secret, right?

The boyfriend. I don't know much about him, and don't care to. I've only ever seen him hanging out by the alley-side door, holding up the wall, always flanked by two other guys. Smoking, spitting, eyeballing passersby. *Spitting*. The boyfriend is a Spitting Guy.

I'll never understand spitting as a final stop, and all the stops along the way that had a hand in making a Spitting Guy—it's a definite type. But he and Deb share his tiny cot every night up on the men's floor. Both of them could get kicked out for it. They know as much but don't seem to care. They have nothing. They have each other.

I make like I'm zipping my lips. Throw away the key. I head into our room—my room for the night.

There's an intimacy between us. Not warmth, certainly—something more desperate. Whatever it is between me and Deb, it appears as an instant. A stay in time. And it's easy to believe in that instant that we might keep one another intact.

Betty and her Bruins games. She's invited me to watch along with her in the office. A wavering rabbit-eared TV fastened with a padlock high up in the corner. And I sit, watching, trying to. It requires I interpret a whole new language *and* follow the puck; a teensy black speck that is never not in rapid motion.

Are the refs unionized?

What's the average age of the players?

Is the Stanley Cup heavy?

And—most importantly—how do I get a job driving the Zamboni?

It must be so satisfying, witnessing your good work as you go, your good work done and put behind you. Every two hours, a clean slate.

But I tamp down my own questions. I keep them to myself.

Smells like snow out. March demands the risk to believe, not exactly my strong suit.

A new-to-me black pea coat from Saint Paul's—it's pill-covered, a bit short in the sleeve with a lining shredded to ribbons, but it looks good. Good and clean. The lady running the coat drive, she needles me when I pluck it from the donation pile. She says, It might be wise to choose something more sensible, don't you think? This isn't a fashion show, after all.

This one like so many, with their compassion measured, even in charity. Like sizing up a panhandler's shoes before tossing them a buck. We should look the part, but not too much. Have some self-respect, and be sure to use this money to get a meal, won't you. This one, with her cashmere twinset, her eyelift, her cloud of Chanel No. 5—handing down the final word on who among us is worthy of care and concern.

But I let it pass. *Go fuck yourself* has been redacted from my vocabulary, at least for the time being.

The off-season streets are uninhabited and gray. A few days earlier they were kelly green. The sun shone. The bars were crammed to maximum capacity, buoyant with curse-chucking day-trippers in town for the Parade. A Newport tradition, a ghastly one.

I've always been content to leave Saint Patrick's Day to the amateurs, even back when I was still drinking. My freckles singled me out among the boorish Kiss Me types—weekend warriors who can't hold their booze. I'm mostly Scottish anyway.

The celebration continued for two days following the Parade, straight through the holiday itself. By now, the piss and vomit has been washed away, the green plastic what-have-you, swept up and thrown into the garbage where it belongs.

Folks from the shelter fuck in the cemetery on Parade Day, Deb tells me. Some unofficial rite of spring. She is very matter-of-fact in the telling, without so much as a passing whiff of judgment.

That's so—*goth*, I say.

Whaddya mean, goth?

It's like … a performance of sadness, kind of. Like, the look of it. Deathly as fashion.

She rolls her eyes in an over-the-top show. College kids, she says. Got too much damn time on their hands.

Except how Mary Shelley lost her virginity at her mother's grave, wore the calcified heart of her dead lover around her neck as a pendant. That's how it's done.

Oh my *goth*, Deb says, smiling. Which is pretty good.

Come summertime, these narrow streets will be clogged once more. At every turn, khaki shorts and flip-flops astride rented bikes. Tourists with feet so tan you might wonder if they'd ever worked a day in their life. When they think of Rhode Island, they think of this. This—*postcard*.

You'd have to squint your eyes. But once you see it, you see it everywhere and cannot un-see. All of us, hidden in plain sight. Even the shelter itself; a concrete block, pale as death, located smack-dab in the touristy fray. Downtown Newport, narrow streets, centuries old, converging in impossibly acute angles.

Maybe they can't see for the looking. Tourists who say Local and it's a barbed word, a word with teeth.

What I should do is, I should tell the social worker he keeps asking the wrong question. That it's not a matter of, do I ever have the urge to drink. It's a matter of, do I ever have the urge to die, even still. The Venn diagram of these two things is a single circle.

People like him, they understand to the extent that they're capable of understanding, which is to say that they don't. They can't. How could they? It wasn't rock bottom like you see on TV. There was no comeuppance or absolution. The story of my relationship with the bottle isn't that kind of story.

Still, moments pass. Days too. And every moment that passes is a moment of something reclaimed. To live as I live now, despite all that is rotten in me and around me—that amounts to something, I suppose. But I don't tell him any of this. What I do is, I shrug. I tell the social worker, No, not really, thank god for little blessings.

It's not that I pity myself. It's just—

It's called an Anniversary Event. A buoy, far offshore, marking the distance to and from. A false estimation of time is called an anachronism. *Mot juste* means the exact, appropriate word.

We might have to cut it short today, the social worker says. The storm's supposed to be a doozy, and on the first day of spring too. He throws his hands up: *New England*, am I right? You're *right. I know*, right?

It's just as well. My birthday always puts me in my place. With its inward eye, where the girl I was twines with the whole year past—with

March and the held-out hope for warmer weather that never seems to come.

Like earlier, headed to the bus stop, heading to the appointment. A sliver of sunlight peeked through the cloud cover. A touch of warmth snuffed out by a gust off the Bay. It slapped my face hard.

The social worker doesn't notice the date, its substance. He's got a few pep talks on heavy rotation, and he sticks to the script. He babbles and my mind goes. I think about things, oddball things. Like how we have parts that can't move towards healing—how teeth can't *get better* with time. Or how born deaf schizophrenics don't hear voices—they see disembodied hands, signing furiously. How a fatal mind knows a single way of being, and that way demands fulfillment.

Focus on how far you've come, is a thing he likes to tell me. But I know enough to know better. Here is what I've come to expect: a malignancy of known patterns; a voice that says I have no one to blame but myself. I suspect it's my mother's voice, lingering.

She has treated me like a drunk—like she's dealing in tough love. But I don't have a drinking problem. I have a living problem, in the sense that I don't want to. Or, I *didn't*. The urge has left me. They call that Recovery too.

The social worker says it's time to take the next step. That it's part of healing to think you can be healed. He hands me a list of shrinks. The paper is warm from the printer and the warmth holds a charge: *It's time to. It's time too.* I thank him and smile; I say see you next month. I give him no indication I will never return.

Could I revive myself if I erased myself? I remember so much, never on purpose. Like the sound of my own voice, teeny and peculiar, calling out for her. There's got to be a word for it—that keystone need for Mother. What do you call a reason *why* that defies all reason?

I'd come close, closest yet. Bandages hugged my forearms. I didn't have to look. The tension of fresh stitches stung from wrist to elbow. They would scar and I was glad for it. There—now it shows.

The curtain parted. A nurse emerged from the blue-white hospital glow.

All I wanted to know was where she was, if they'd gotten in touch with her yet.

The nurse approached my bedside, clasped my hand with both of hers. Her delivery was gentle: Your mother isn't coming; she doesn't want to see you.

I knew there was more, that I was spared the details of what my mother *really* said. Something about selfishness and sob stories, how everyone's got problems; what made me think I'm so special?

The nurse said she was sorry. I asked her what for. She told me no one chooses this, that I was not to blame. I took little breaths and managed a nod. Silence fell between us and held us close together. The nurse called me Sweetie, released my hand, and left.

It's been a year—one year to the day. I remember every day since.

I've got a job now, a job and a place to stay. And both should set me right, enough that I could regain. But my nature is constant and makes itself known. It's as if a bird flew straight into my chest, right into the center, and got stuck there. As if the bird were flapping its wings madly, blowing my chest apart in an effort to get free.

What I want is to feel as little as possible. The meds, in theory, help me manage.

I still see the bearded brain doc at the mental health clinic, of course I do. I take the pills because he tells me to. I still don't have health insurance, of course I don't, but I get my meds filled at the clinic for free. I feel terrible, yes, but not unhinged. Life insists I am just like this now, and so I act accordingly.

Riding the bus is a comfort, how it moves in one direction. I train my eyes out the window. A familiar blur of gas stations, coffee shops, and pizza joints. Twilight deepens. The interior light turns on and stays on. My reflection appears in the glass.

It starts to fall. Slow at first, then faster and faster. Broad wet flakes that will make a mess. Each headlight and streetlight, a birthday candle flickering in the springtime snow.

A woman gets on in Warren and takes the seat beside me. She's workday weary, she's had it up to *here*. But her bare legs draw my attention—plump and pale and peppered with razor burn. The fluttering hem of a floral dress peeks out from under her woolen parka, just below the knee.

I see her, how she understands all that I've forgotten. Winter always turns to spring.

This life must be a test I am taking. Unless the test is to see how much I can take.

Deb clucks her tongue. However you're doing it, Ro, it is a good way to do it. Because you's here, ain't you?

And don't say hate, she says. Hate's not a nice thing to say.

Fine—I dislike it to the maximum.

Doing something by doing nothing is a thing I could do. I could stay in Newport—stay where I landed, stay where I fell. Beats my life of same, same, same. The scene of the crime on every corner, crime scenes every which way.

By the time I ditched out of the emergency room back in June, I could see it all unfolding just as it had before. How it would lead me back to pre-dawn vitals, mewling cries, a slow-rolling Lithium shuffle in treaded socks. How nothing would change, I wouldn't change, because I could no longer remember when things had ever been any other way. But it did but I didn't and still I can't.

If you ever feel unsafe, I had been told, just walk into the ER and say so.

They cared nothing for the details of my compromised life, and who could blame them. Fine, they would keep me kept, if only in service to the nebulous good.

The sliding glass door had required a badge to enter, a simple swipe of say-so. But anyone could leave. I yanked the port from my thin skin, raised the blood to my lips. The mark soon enough bloomed black.

Maybe I would do well, staying in the system. Most of the long-timers here at the shelter are up to their eyeballs in the system, Deb included. And what of it?

We're all doing the best we can do—there has never been a time when we weren't doing the best we could do.

I come upon the scene by the stairwell as it's wrapping up. Deb is distraught, screaming into another woman's face. It's called incontinence, you bitch, and it's not funny!

I don't have to know what happened to know what happened. The picture is pretty clear.

Imagine yourself falling deeply in love with someone, only to find out they believe in ghosts, they clap when the movie ends or they live to torture waitresses. What I mean is, it could always be worse, Deb.

She knuckles her tears away and says, My ex saw a ghost once, and he wasn't that bad.

She's closer to sixty than not, but times like this, I glimpse the little girl she was—or the little girl she could have been, were it not for everything else. That's the thing with Deb, with all of us here. The thing beneath the thing.

She says, You know what I wish? More than anything? It's something heartbreaking, the thing she wishes for.

She's sleeping the sleep of the dead when I return from the mini mart. I hide a surprise in the sleeve of her parka. A pack of smokes and those crumbly coffee cakes she loves. I will already be gone by the time she finds them tomorrow.

No parting words, no fake plans or false promises to stay in touch. Some call it a French Exit, or an Irish Goodbye. Not me, but some people.

The Townie Split: it's my signature move.

SUMMER

I AM ON THE FLOOR

The air mattress has emptied slowly through the night. This is fine, I say aloud to no one.

I've fled into the arms of Pawtucket, into a two-room studio less than a mile from where I was born. A decision deprived of any meaning, as far as I'm concerned. Beggars can't be choosers. I am doing what I can.

You know how certain places grow more powerful in the mind with the passing of time? Yeah, me neither.

Lockdown drills and gonorrhea outbreaks at my old high school. The principal arrested for possession of child pornography. My old weed dealer, that troglodyte grab-ass—he's a local cop now.

Look away, folks. Nothing to see here!

A young woman dives from her Subaru, barely managing to throw it into park. Ambushes me on the sidewalk, introducing herself. She's one of them, I can tell, and maybe she thinks I am one of them too. The artists and musicians abandoning Providence, moving to Pawtucket, trying to get a scene going, trying to make Pawtucket a thing. Everything is changing, it's true, but people rarely change. Pawtucket, I know, will push back.

So, where're you from? she says.

Here.

No, I mean, where were you raised?

Here. Right here.

Where'd you go to school, then?

Didn't.

Ugh, that's so punk rock, the young woman says, smiling.

But she works in an office drafting grant proposals. I work in a stockroom.

In a fit of optimism, I purchased a bureau and a hulking TV set from the previous tenant. Thirty bucks for the two. I have nothing to fill the bureau, but I might. No—I will.

And how did I become a cat person? They left their cat behind. They just *left her*. Now she is mine. Now she's named Dot.

I am okay, but I am not well. Left to my own devices, a ringing doorbell might be the end of me, might be the very thing that does me in.

There—an unannounced visitor did the job you could never manage!

That's me, speaking to myself. Speaking to my fucking scars. The ones you can see, the ones you can't.

All in all, there are two rules in the Program: don't drink, and go to meetings. The simplicity is appealing. That, and how the Program loves an aphorism. The best one is, You're only as sick as your secrets.

I continue going to meetings, but there are no answers for me in those seated circles. I don't even keep track of the time that has passed. It's been how long without a hangover? No use celebrating, no need to pat me on the back. It is not virtuous to not do the thing I do not want to do.

What keeps one foot in front of the other is selective remembering. Selective forgetting. Like how I don't go to the library anymore because it is brimming with all that has passed.

The bathroom where I had washed up, where I took a breather

or took a nap. The green reading room with the green reading lamps. The fiction stacks, all my friends lined up in a row. I might smell the familiar smells; I might see the familiar sights. Yet something essential has changed. Like I've lost myself and gained empty space for the losing.

So—I am gathering cracked spines, underlined passages, and dog-eared pages. I am buying up used books, as many as I can. As if I could live inside them. I will stack the odds in my favor. I will stack them all around me. My bookcase deities. I will buy a bookcase, cheap.

I bolt my door at night, every night. The irony of it. Me, making nice with notions of safety and control. Me, who lived so long with the steady urge of a mind that wanted me dead.

Here's the movie I want to see: A killer breaks into the home of a broken, fatal-minded woman, and is greeted as a conquering hero. *Finally*, she says, and puts on some Elliot Smith.

These little red pills coax me on. Better than coffee and diet soda and energy drinks combined, plus my sinuses are wrung dry. But I've been cut off at the pharmacy. I have to wait until next month. I really flipped out on the pharmacists. Went full-tilt riled-up dirtbag, and proved their point in doing so—they're right to keep the cold medicine behind the counter now.

You're not going to like this, I tell Dot. It's nothing personal.

I flutter my feet beneath the blanket. She jumps from my lap to the floor, follows me into the bathroom just to sit and glare. It's like she doesn't believe me. When I say I am sorry. When I say I'll be right back. There was a time when people trusted me. I wouldn't leave me alone either.

Hunting something unseen. So is the cat. I find it in my shoe, eviscerated. What had I expected? That maybe Dot would just rough it up a bit. Like—don't come around here no more, and tell your friends the same!

I wrap it carefully in toilet paper, as if preparing it for a teeny pyre. But the murdered mouse is tossed without ceremony into the storm drain on my way to the bus stop. Let the rainwater take it to Valhalla, I'm late for work.

And then another one. My sweet fuzzy Dot, a totally sick fuck. Except she doesn't kill it outright, just mortally wounds it. Scampers away, invulnerable, and curls up on the air mattress for a nap. But the mouse is still breathing. I see its chest rising and falling from where I stand. Vomiting comes as a surprise, hard and fast. A dead mouse—okay, fine. A dying mouse, it turns out, is all too much.

It's not that I feel bad for myself. Not in the slightest. A grownup is someone who is always upset. Misery as a rite of adulthood—the only rite that matters. A lesson from my upbringing, growing up in the shadow of a forlorn mill town. The weight of Pawtucket crushing us all.

Like how some parents have ideas: My children will have the opportunities I never had.

And yet—I *work* for a living, the parents always say.

They say, Let me tell ya something. And it's always something terrible.

They say, I wish someone told me when I was your age. … And it's always something brutal, the thing they wish someone told them.

The ability to take a beating. It's not nothing.

Get in your room and shut your mouth, my mother would hiss. Your father's downstairs paying bills. The coded phrase our little bodies could translate.

I look into my face reflecting. I say, You're fine, everything's fine. It was a rough patch, is all. But a phantom paces behind my irises. Get me out of here, I whine, and what I am talking about is my body.

Me and myself are in constant dialogue. The conversation is going nowhere. These voices think they have my best interest at heart—can you imagine? They step up to the mic as if they're not an attribute of my self. As if they're the whole shebang.

My urge to hurt myself never left. I know because I smoke in bed. All night smoking, not sleeping.

I am the highly suggestible type. Infomercials, they work on me. I want it all, but especially the food dehydrator. I delight in the idea. A world of turkey jerky and watermelon fruit roll-ups is the world I want to live in. So much better than this world of mine: Diet Coke twelve-packs, an oven filled with used paperbacks, ashtrays balanced on stacked up phone books. The phone books are really something. They won't, stop, coming.

How hypnotic is my sleeplessness? I imagine myself joining a cult, but a new one that's just getting off the ground, when everyone is riding high and living with purpose. Before the polygamy, the child abuse, the demanded liquidation of personal assets. There's always a pink cloud era in these cults, however brief. I'm an easy mark. That kind of crushing certainty. It sure is appealing.

Me and 4 a.m. Existentialism. It's a torrid love affair; an outgrowth of what is normal to my nature. Why do I exist? Or—*since* I exist, now what? Why should there be something to live for instead of nothing? I could just as easily ask the opposite. Maybe nothing is the natural state of things, and something would be weird. Really though? It doesn't matter.

But I'll see you in hell, person on my block who's been screaming on the street for an hour now. Don't they know some of us have alarms to snooze? Some of us have buses to run for. Buses to miss, excuses to make.

And that racket overhead, stomping feet, furniture being moved in the middle of the night. My upstairs neighbor, conjuring fresh ways to ruin my life.

&

My anxiety is the *stare at the wall* kind of anxiety. And my coffee habit is the *by the vat* kind. These two form a formidable pair. Their powers combined consume hours of my day. Left to languish on a day off from work, I don't inhabit my body before noon. What it means for me is—why bother with TV when you can watch your wheels turn?

Baby blue eye shadow, probably a stay-over from something she heard once, a way to make blue eyes pop.

A knock-off designer handbag that passed well as the real thing. Extra money spent to ensure the counterfeit tell was on the inside.

Sun-damaged skin across her nose and cheeks.

A face round as mine. My face, a face round as hers.

I scan her as she appears in my mind but I cannot make out her shoes. There's nothing south of the ankle. I focus real hard but her shoes do not appear.

Sandals in the summer, I think. Maybe.

To that end, she'd say something like, how could I've forgotten that ankle boots or loafers or whatever the fuck else were her thing, how my forgetting means I never knew her at all. Image is what matters to my mother, and it is all that remains. What's missing means more than the image of the thing itself.

Thing, not person. What, not who.

It's a stretch to imagine. A hand on my head. A comforting embrace. A muffled voice whispering, I love you no matter what. It's a stretch.

What I have is the contented engine of my cat. I long to see myself as she sees me.

A scene from an alternate reality might look like:

A waitress asking, No Pepsi—is Coke okay?

A guy seated beside me on the bus asking, Got enough room?

A phone call from my mother asking, How you holding up?

I am sick and tired of thinking about her.

In the Program, they say the change happens when you're sick and tired of being sick and tired.

Halfway there.

I could maximize on those things I have control over. That is a thing I could do.

I've discovered that the battleship-gray floor paint in my kitchen has been done over so many times it peels off in long, easy strips. So that's what I'll be doing this evening.

Shouldn't I take pride in my surroundings now that I have a place of my own? I've considered it, yes. But womb-like comfort is what I'm after. A womb with a view. Did I mention my apartment has a view? A sweeping vista of a gym parking lot?

Here is some stuff I like is my design aesthetic. I've gone and kissed my security deposit goodbye, wheat-pasting magazine cutouts onto the wall. I'm pretty much one Bob Marley poster shy of a freshman dorm room. It's like that.

So, I live like a boxcar hobo. But I can translate my own disarray. Like I know I will find my coffee mug on the bathroom sink because that's my last stop before I shoot out the door, late for work. Thinking along those lines, everything makes sense. Nothing is ever out of order. Nothing ever goes lost.

I'm locked in an endless feedback loop of reactions; it's true. But I can make a deliberate choice. I don't feel like I can, it doesn't seem like I can, but I have experience to draw upon. Like that time I rolled on Ecstasy while wearing red pleather pants, understanding those pleather pants might never come off.

Better to find consolation in a place—this place, my place—than in *stuff*. When I lament the loss of all my *stuff*, I try to remember there's power in it. How no one worth knowing would ever say, I'm so glad I still have those red pleather pants I wore back when I was twenty. I can be the person worth knowing in this scenario.

See—now is the time for guts and guile. But all I'm asking for is the nerve to tell the cashier at the pizza joint she has made a mistake with my order.

I'm splintering. Summertime now, and the windows are open. I wonder, Do the people passing by on the sidewalk hear me talking to my cat? I ask my cat to weigh-in, but Dot is grumpy and particular and I respect her boundaries. I close the windows just in case.

There are always familiar faces on the bus to and from work; those of us who are on the same timetable. But I keep my head down. I am not above telling a person, Sorry I do not want to talk to you. Only twice has someone called me a bitch in response.

He keeps my attention, though. No joke, his name is Romeo— Romeo the boxer. Or so he says. He works at the mall like me, at the vitamin store, selling legal speed and legal steroids and strange chalky powders. I've seen him around, I tell him, and he says he's seen me too; that I'm hard to miss. I like his crooked nose and every last beating it implies.

I feel his eyes on my skin, gliding, and I feel his eyes peel away. In the white morning light, in the hot summer heat, my purple seams are raised and angry from wrist to elbow. They look like what they are.

Oh, these? I walked into a sliding glass door when I was a kid, and some other self-deprecating nonsense, something about clumsiness.

He laughs a nervous little machine gun laugh, offers up a quip of his own. For the rest of the ride, the silence we share is an awkward one.

And now I have to go up a floor, box around, and take the escalator back down again just to get a coffee from Dunkin' Donuts. I have to avoid the vitamin store—I have to take an earlier bus.

In the play, Romeo was a whiny weasel. Juliet was the one with balls. Gave herself a knife to the heart, for chrissakes, and that's no small thing.

I couldn't get off even if I wanted to. I have dead pussy and it feels like relief. One less thing, you know?

The Olympics offer two weeks worth of something to look at. I like the racing sports best. There's nothing subjective, only a time. You're either the fastest, or you're not. I don't consider myself competitive, no. I just have a hankering to be the best, even if it's the best worst ever.

My take away from the closing ceremony spectacle is, the host country sure has tremendous control over their people.

Lawnmowers and leaf blowers and someone somewhere discordantly pounds a hammer.

Since January, I have limped towards summer: Everything will be better come summertime! But I hide with the shades drawn and the windows closed. Sweating, muttering, wondering when it was that my outsides came to match my insides.

Shoveling, putting up Christmas lights, raking and mowing, ripping up the ivy. I was the biggest. I had to help. The ivy was really something. It grew back with a vengeance year after year. Weaving in and out of the aluminum siding, thriving in the shade. By August, it covered the garage from top to bottom.

My father, swearing and ripping, refusing to wear gloves. Me, gathering and piling, stuffing the vines into sturdy brown lawn bags.

It'll take over the whole damn house, my father would grumble.

That kind of tenacity—he took it personally.

I prayed, Grant me the resilience of a climbing plant. But I am a human animal, brutally aware, born to freeze. I used to be a fighter. Now—not so much.

And there are the migraines to contend with. Scenes from a life lived, a denouement rolling out on the backs of my eyelids, exploding behind my face. I see auras, except I do not believe in auras. But what the hell do I know, what, with my pupils dilated in mismatched sizes. There is no range of motion in which to find comfort.

The salve of darkness, at last, and I open a window. Outside it smells of plants at night—summer humidity, green life.

I SAW A SIGN

The sign was posted in the break room. So I threw my hat into the ring, so what. It's fluff, though, not even a promotion at all. I won't make any more than I make hauling stock, breaking down boxes. But yes, of course I inquired. Because I am a fish, a big dumb fish drawn to the sparkling and dangling and altogether useless aspects of this daily slog. Operating from the outside, in—it has its appeal. So, yes, it's an unlikely promotion, maybe even unprecedented in the lifetime of Filene's department store. A bump from the stockroom to Cosmetics. But I suppose stranger things have happened.

This counter is for the apple-cheeked, the freshly-scrubbed, the no-makeup makeup set. And I'm not into it, really. I'd like to be aligned with a more creative brand, a real makeup-y makeup brand. But there's a compliment in there somewhere, as if my diligent sunscreen use has paid off.

How *I don't care if I live or die* and *I'm going to live forever* sometimes manifest identically. Refusing to floss, for example. Guzzling whiskey, guzzling diet soda. And yet I always wore sunscreen.

The Cosmetics Department is a mix of bawdy old biddies, and the very young. No one is in between. I like the old broads best. They love to talk shit and they don't suffer fools.

The young ones are college-aged part-timers. They talk about partying in coded phrases they think they've invented. I never let on that I know better, that they're not as clever as they think, that if they knew my partying stories they would lose their minds. I'm happy to throw them a bone.

The old broads are keen to offer advice. Don't drink your coffee straight from the cup—use a straw, it will preserve your lipstick. Don't use a straw—it will give you lip lines worse than a smoking habit.

We all smoke. We take our smoke breaks together. That's their advice in a nutshell: You're screwed no matter what.

I can see myself doing all the things I do not do, but should:

Getting out of bed at the first cry of my alarm.

Drinking water, taking vitamins, eating a goddamn vegetable.

Carrying on, playing along. Forcefully forgetting.

Acting the good daughter by never ever looking back.

Keeping what happened in that house locked away in that house forever.

I should do this, I shouldn't think that. I think of my shoulds all the time, shoulding all over myself. I cannot moderate all these shoulds. I'm not running a support group here. Everyone's voice doesn't count. Get bent, shoulds.

Like an idiot, I keep trying. She will pick up on the fourth ring when I call, as if she weighed the pros and cons of answering. She will say, Hello? as if she cannot see that it's me who is calling.

Oh. Hello, Rosemary.

I will fill the space breathlessly. I will tell her all about my promotion—I could probably get you a discount, I say—but she will cut me off. She always has an appointment. My mother always has to let me go.

Nothing is more contagious than a bad old idea. Used to be my general attitude was akin to, let's just drink all the booze or do all the drugs so that once we're done, there won't be any more drugs and booze left, and we won't have to worry about self-control.

But I don't drink, don't do drugs, not anymore. Wouldn't say no to some weed, though. I cannot, however, have ice cream in the house. Or chips. Or even cough syrup, for that matter.

Hindsight and whatnot: So much time wasted in my youth, worrying I might accidentally smoke Angel Dust. There were other things I should've been worried about.

What is it like, I wonder, to have known only good times with your mind? The good-natured trust of someone delighted to think their thoughts?

That's my beef with most people. Probably why I don't have any friends. How could I possibly trust the good in people when I hate most people?

Or maybe my job is poisoning me. Already. Retail is a wasting disease.

Then again, it isn't work if it isn't hard. That's why I use skincare products that hurt a little, so I know something's happening.

There is an animal growing inside me. A subliminal sense of wanting more than what I've come to expect. Wanting more expression and redefinition in order to, what? Rip everything to shreds.

They say depression is anger turned inward. Festering anger.

I can't hear over the rattling between my ears. Good thing, though, for there is no need. My days are populated with interactions in which there is no real interaction. Touching nothing, nothing touching me. Airless bubbles bumping up against one another ever so politely.

The cashier at the sandwich place asks, Do you want your receipt?

No, don't worry, I'm not going to return it.

Ha, ha.

A customer asks, How much is this moisturizer? There's no price tag.

I guess that means it's free.

Ha, ha.

Everything is changing shape, becoming something else.

The brain doc at the clinic, he marvels at my sobriety—like that is the only goal and aim. And how I've got a job and a place to stay. I get it, you know—*considering*. But he pays no mind to the fine line I walk. He's just another person I can fool into believing I am real and here.

It's an odd experience when you and your prognosticator are the same age. In certain circles, a peer. All the pop cultural influences of their adolescence snap into place and, in an instant: Oh, I see who you are. You're that guy. I always hated that guy.

I nod to the bookcase spanning the wall behind his desk. You really read all those?

I'm sure I did. Yes—yes, *of course* I did.

But I am dubious and he can tell.

You, you're really something, aren't you, Rosemary.

This, I know, is not a compliment. He will not be challenged, not by the likes of me. With all my admissions and broken bonds, my sheer fucking audacity.

He speaks carefully. His words, both hammer and nail. You are an emotional genius, he says. But with a tone daring me to uncover the insult.

This is the dance we do. I watch him watching me. He sees me watching him watch me, and I become his adversary in this game where I know none of the rules, hold none of the cards, and have everything to lose.

Maybe my problem is a problem of translation. Or maybe I am wrong. I've been wrong about a lot of things.

Rooms are opening up in my memory. They are in the shape of me. Me as I am now and all the me's I have ever been. They are the containers into which I have been poured.

Nightmares I do not remember, a signal sounding from deep, dark water. Miles below, something has come alive. I wake up sheeted with sweat. The sweat smells primal; smells like acrid fear.

There were times when I failed to distinguish between the memory of something I had read and the memory of something that had happened to me. This is no longer the case.

I describe my mind as a rusty filing cabinet in furious disarray— beyond reconciliation, even. The filing cabinet has been emptied and reordered.

Everything is available to me now, whether I like it or not. The more time passes the sharper they become, memories more real, more precise, than the life I am living.

The doctor stitches his eyebrows, appears to stifle a laugh. You're just so eager to tell your story all of a sudden, he says, that arrogant bearded fuck. And he looks off, out the window beyond the rattling whir of North Main Street, grasping for the memory of something he once was told. Instructional feedback about bedside manner, non-judgment, applied compassion, how he would do well to implement some goddamned empathy.

Sounds like PTSD, is what he says. As if it were a chest cold, a stomach bug, something minimal that will abate with time.

But what of it? All of this, meaning most of me, is relegated to shit because it—I—have no real utility. There's no name for what I am. Just as there's no real reason for why I have carried on.

What I lack is access to the ordinary. This is not an original concept. I did not invent alienation. And yet—

The doctor scribbles and hands me a paper script. I translate his well-practiced chicken scratch. No, I tell him. This—*this* turned me to rubber last time. Rubber can't live in the world. Rubber can't keep a job.

If I could sit in the sun for a while I might be able to sort myself out. I'd let myself be cooked. The sun, a star, a perpetual nuclear explosion. I should be so lucky, burned by starlight. But here, it rains. The weather report, one week at a glance, seven little gray clouds in a row.

It's another antipsychotic; the crowd controlling kind: slow 'em down, thicken 'em up, turn 'em dull as cattle. That, and the huge angular tabs I call trapezoids, which is horseshoes-close to what they're really called. What the trapezoids do is they eliminate consciousness. I go out like a million lights. There is no rest, just a weighted feeling directly followed by the splitting scream of my alarm. Now I hate going to sleep because going to sleep means waking up, which means work.

I miss it now that it's gone. Those hollow nights, waiting for the light to appear outside my window. It was something I could count on.

But I take the pills because he has told me to take them. It's something; a proactive thing. My weight is ballooning. My tits are sore and I cannot cry. Tears build behind my eyes but the tears never come.

I long for the days when I felt no need to tell people the truth about myself; when I invented whole histories without so much as a passing flicker of guilt.

Flaming out as an exploding star, these fictions did the job of cultivating my undoing.

I imagine white-coated doctors looking down over me, administering an invented origin story—*drip*—or an imagined job history—*drip, drip*—or even a name. She's comfortable, one of them would say. It's just a matter of time now.

I know the power of a lie. And others would do well with inhabiting that power too. Like in the song "Long Black Veil." Why didn't they just say they were planning a surprise party?

What I did was, I stacked them up all around me, and then I hid inside. A pack of lies for which I feel no shame. Even still, not even now. There was nothing malicious, not as I saw it. Only the simple comforts of watching myself recede, an entirely different individual stepping to the fore. Mobilized by whiskey—lots.

When I told those strangers whatever it is I told them, I could actually see the patterns of the life I had described, but from up on high looking down, growing larger—a plane descending, a plane crashing. As if I were aware of my ability to pass, in their eyes, as an ordinary, intact woman. Young woman. Girl. I gave myself away when it was all I had to offer. When in time I was revealed as what I am—lost, broken, etcetera, etcetera—the ubiquitous Other would flash with anger. They had been duped! And for what?

That's how it went down with the Old Bastard. I took pleasure in spelling it out for him.

So, you're *not* a successful painter then.

Why would a successful anyone spend time with *you*?

Oh, what the art of a lie reveals about the truth of a life. I barely registered his punch. I remember only that I hit back—harder.

And, fuck me, I just handed it to them, didn't I? The ability to say, I knew her until the day she died.

Maybe that's the appeal with the promotion, the makeup, the mirrored surfaces, and the bright white lights. The look of it all. I can disguise myself from those who consider me long dead.

AUTUMN

I AM TETHERED
TO MY FATHER

A rope tied tightly around my waist, the same rope tied tightly around his. He stands at the edge of a cliff, toes curled over as if it were a diving board.

I see him looking not out or down, but over his shoulder. Looking at me.

He doesn't say a word because he doesn't have to.

The threat is in the tautness of the rope. No slack whatsoever.

This is a lie. It's real, but real as a poem is real. I do not dream dreams like this.

I stretch out into the multiverse. I live alternate realities, something that might have come to pass had I made a different choice, had I chosen a different path or had a different path chosen me. My mind does not conjure anything that couldn't happen. Fantastic is not in my makeup. I'm forced to live in the world as it is, even in dreams.

Like when I dreamed I had effectively flushed my phone down the toilet. It was a gesture. An action meant to signify—what?

Doesn't matter. My mornings usually lack promise. It was a good dream.

&

I thought I was psychic when I was a girl. Used to be the dreamer, dreaming, could glean the answers to questions never asked. The part of me that felt so much knew things without knowing how or why, just knew in the way you just know.

I set out writing down my dreams upon waking to gauge what would or would not come true—namely, to test my powers. Except the dreams left me as I reached for them. The tighter I closed my fist around them, the more they slipped through my fingers.

I made one up to see what would happen, a dream where pigs flew through a whiteout snowstorm, through the pages of my journal. My real journal, a black and white composition notebook, not the decoy I kept for my mother, tucked between my mattress and box spring. That one I filled with Dear Diary bullshit, just enough to throw her off the scent.

The knowingness left me. Slowly, then all at once, it was replaced by the dread of everything and nothing. Something I felt but could not name.

I came to dedicate more time to the decoy rather than my real journal. I wrote about quizzes and Christmas wish lists, the hope of drawing some boy's attention, all in fat rounded handwriting I had cribbed from the girls in my class. I's dotted with perfect circles, lots of exclamation points.

The world I inhabited on those pale pink pages was a world wholly different from my own. Play-acting a sense of normal I had never known: I am safe, I am safe, this place is a home.

Girls plunder whatever modes and forms they require. They do what they can. That was me, doing what I could. The wolf wasn't at the door, but in the house.

A phone call from my father.

How am I? How am I. I'm fine, I tell him, and answer banal

questions about my job, about myself, as if I am not perpetually at risk of losing my job and myself.

See, Rosie? I knew you'd grow out of it. It was just a rough patch, is all. I'm always saying, some lessons gotta be learned the hard way, y'know? I mean, look at yous now.

That's my friend on the other line, I lie. I have to go.

My phone rings four hours later. Him again, but this time sent to voicemail. A five-minute message. He's hammered, weeping like a clown.

They say *lapsed Catholic* as if it somehow got away from you. But a Catholic is always a Catholic, whether they go to church or not. What they're dealing in is guilt. Guilt like sand. Guilt that gets into everything.

My father will not remember. Outside of a blackout, he has access to resentment, inferiority—nothing more. Anything else emerges only when he's deep in his cups.

I won't remember this either. I outright refuse. Delete, delete, delete.

I'll tell you one thing. I will not anger-cut my own bangs; I will not.

I funnel all of myself into this process instead, making a mix tape so I can congratulate myself on my impeccable taste in music. Me, song after song, saying aloud: Oh, I love this song. Let me have this. I need it.

Can I just say something? I say.

No—you don't get to know better, I say.

I should be so lucky. If I were truly a multiple, maybe I wouldn't feel all alone.

So, for now the bathtub is a good place for me. The empty bathtub.

Which self-help guy do you mean? the bookseller asks.

The famous one. The one with the weird name and weird speaking voice.

The book cautions against practicing this particular meditation without a teacher, which is the most hippie nonsense hippie nonsense I have ever heard. I'm not looking for love and light. I just want to kick this claustrophobia. I just want my skin to fit again.

I sit in my mind, in the empty little room, as I've done a million times before. Just wait until your father gets home, my mother would say, snarling through her teeth. A clock ticking, a hinge creaking, a body filling the doorway, a pair of boots staggering across the carpet.

How I realize I am incapable of using fear to bend a living thing to my will: I bought an empty spray bottle in an effort to reign-in Dot. She's up on every surface, she has pooped on the floor—she is drunk with power. A spritz of water at any infraction will reinstitute my authority. Or so I've read.

As she walks along the counter, threading through the lipstick-marked mugs, the dirty plates and half-emptied Diet Coke cans, I spray her right in her little face.

For twenty minutes, I am crouched on the kitchen floor, trying to coax her out from behind the fridge.

I'm sorry I'm sorry I'm sorry I'm sorry.

Autumn arrives, not with the leaves turning, but sooner. With sunlight gone from bright white to buttery, a breeze rattling in the bushes by my window, mornings wrung free from humidity.

And the students.

The school year has barely begun, yet the art student across the hall is recovering from a suicide attempt. I know because I can smell my own. A person willing their phantom torment into the walking, talking world, coaxing their secret self to the surface.

That, and the ambulance come and gone the other night. The young woman screaming *Please!* and *Don't!* through his dead-bolted door.

I envy him. I hate myself for it. It's the well-wishers. They arrive every hour, solemn, sometimes in pairs. One looked old enough to be a professor and I like to think she was. A thoughtful mentor, eager to help, whispering, I am so glad you're here.

His parents never appear and I suspect that's by design. A failed attempt kept under wraps. My first time, I failed in a way that no one would ever know. That, too, was by design.

Are you feeling unsafe?

Do you have a plan?

Would you say so if you did?

Better yet: When did you first picture your own death?

What did you see?

These are not considerations but convictions. Both my onus and my ease.

That nurse who told me, No one chooses this; that I was not to blame. I had no receptors for the message she carried. It wasn't in me to hear all she had to say.

All pain is real pain.

The lessons appear in the strangest places. Sometimes across the hall. The locked door you see as you first step into the world each morning, running late for work.

It's always fall out when I think of my Grammy and Pop Pop. It's always fall out and there's always a leaf fire burning somewhere. It's always fall out and there's always Mary Jane peanut chews or Peach Blossom ribbon candy.

Pop Pop taught me to read. My memory of him smells like library books. He died when I was five, and Grammy moved down to Southern Florida. Went to the Chrysler dealer straight away, lied about her age, and leased a brand-new car. A gold LeBaron convertible with maroon leatherette interior. She loved that car. I loved *her* in that car. Her Patsy

Cline tape, her white bouffant bobbing along with the walking bass line. Tan fingers gripping the wheel, fuchsia manicure carving half-moons into her palms. Right foot on the gas, left foot on the brake, dancing back and forth between the two.

Every year, she made the drive up for the holidays with ripe tomatoes and navel oranges riding shotgun. They would've rotted by the time she finally made it to Rhode Island, filling the LeBaron with the smell of sunshine gone bad.

After Grammy died, my mother became quite the storyteller. Her tales were positioned for a laugh: Grammy as her adversary, always striking first but easily outwitted, won over with flattery. My mother was never a girl in the stories she told. Nothing hurt and no one was to blame and it was all in good fun.

Years added up, distancing her from Grammy's death, and my mother's stories changed. Rosy ribbing gave way to hard-nosed disdain.

Who's laughing now, and what have we learned?

A family legacy. Inherited ways. A debt to be paid in full.

When I told my mother I wanted to die, she said she didn't want to hear it. Shaking her head, reaching for indignation. She said I was selfish, that I only thought about myself. She walked to her bedroom down the hall, closed the door behind her. Didn't look back. An electric fence activated between us. We'd never be on the same side again.

Accepting the consequences of my ... let's call them *tendencies*. Or, at the very least, bracing myself for the consequences. All this, masquerading as self-awareness.

Que será.

The cave you fear to enter holds the treasure that you seek. I read it again, aloud. Dot gives me a nonplussed look with one eye squeezed shut.

Listen, I tell her. And I mean business.

You will die some day, I say. What I mean is, I know how this sounds, but I really think you're going to live forever.

I want to be well, yes. But I want vengeance too. I am desperate to prove to them I have been right all along. I need evidence of—what?

This world of revelations.

FEAR OF LOSS

It's a selling strategy. It means get it while you can.

But everyone shows up at this job with clean hair like they got all the answers. It bears repeating: if I can't remember the last time I took a shower, well then it's time to lather the hell up already.

This can't be returned, I tell the customer. You can't return an empty bottle.

I unscrew the top, turn the bottle upside down. See? Gone. Not even a drop.

I want, my, money back, the customer hisses.

The bottle is empty, ma'am. If I refund your money, you will have stolen this body lotion. If you're okay with that, with *stealing*, well ...

Apoplectic is the right word here. Belligerent. Just, loud.

I'm sorry to hear that, I lie.

She can take her business elsewhere, that's fine. I make nine dollars an hour. She can see herself out.

My boss is waiting for me behind the counter when I return from break. The department manager. The HR manager too. It's time we have a talk, they say as one.

Now I've gone ahead and ruined everything.

As is my way.

I make nothing easier for myself, ever.

And what have we learned?

Mine is an un-girdled, sprawling, expansive self-betrayal.

She had choked on the words. You are … *unwell*, the HR manager said, all in her throat. And she wasn't wrong.

It's affecting team morale, the department manager added.

I'm not sure that I, alone, can be blamed for team morale—

Irregardless, she said.

If you've ever wondered whether crazy people know they're crazy, I'm here to tell you we don't. We only recognize the getting there part, and only some of the time.

All of us in this room, we're not cutie pie kooky, manic pixie whatever the hell. Our very presence here indicates that our way of seeing the world is just wrong, that everything we do is a behavior we might want to stop. I am not the only one whose hand has been forced.

It was a deal I struck with the brain doc at the clinic. Either in- or out-, he said, that fucker. Either in-patient or out-. He gave me a say in the matter. Which is new; which is different.

They call it the partial hospital, but these are classes. We're in a classroom, blackboard and all. For maybe the first time ever, I am part of a group that will have me. A group of women, only women, learning how to sit with discomfort. How to bite down on the leather strap. How to grin and bear it.

Distress tolerance. That's what we get, that's the best we can expect. The idea is that we might notice what is happening to us; that there is no situation in which we are excluded from our own lives.

The classroom has a palpable sense of catastrophe. We are vibrating as one.

There's Snappish Cathy complaining about her state job.

Load-mouthed Cassie who talks over everyone.

Hissing Angela who wants to speak to the person in charge.

Quiet Margie, thick-tongued from Lithium.

Snarling Donna, going off about her seven-year-old granddaughter: She acts like she thinks she's better than everyone, Snarling Donna says.

It's easy for me to see myself as these women see me. I wear red lipstick one time and, from then on out, they call me Your Majesty.

We pay a price to live like this. We've paid a price to live.

It seems to be that the world called us into existence, us crazy bitches.

Sometimes it's just a matter of predisposition, the counselor says.

Which brings me right back to feeling born-rotten.

Like how a person says, I love you. And we scoff: *Aren't you embarrassed?*

How a person says, I hate you. And we take their word for it: Yeah, that checks out.

I ought to paint my walls with two words repeated over and over: And yet. Huge, festering *And yet*'s dogging me at every turn. Because, try as I might, I cannot break loose. I keep one foot in front of the other, yes, but I don't feel traction beneath my feet. Where at once I could advance, I always retrograde.

The hollow feeling of a Sunday all the time, knowing what will follow, how things get worse but never seem to get better. That *60 Minutes* clock, counting down to god knows what else.

And how hard is it, resisting the urge to tell the counselor, this child leading the group, to go fuck herself? It's not nothing.

The youngest one, Loud-mouthed Cassie, she goes right ahead entertaining the most useless speculation of all:

If I was a man…

And, appropriately, she trails off. Because none of us would be here if we were men. None of us would be. We would've gotten used to helping ourselves by now; helping ourselves to others. How these men, these boys grown old, carry on as if they're both invincible and persecuted. How they've got it all figured out in a world itching to get one over on them.

The men on the Incurable Ward, they sprawled. They spread themselves out over couches and chairs. They put up their feet, they'd had a long day. And there was always one in the fullest expression of mania, always belligerent, kinetic, and loud. But he had withstood a respectable kind of brutality, we were told, so the manic man was given a wide berth.

I'm not like you, he'd shout. And he was right. But he was wrong.

Quiet Margie, fiddling with the bandage around her left forearm, making excuses for her dirtbag boyfriend. He means well, she mumbles.

And you, what? *Don't?*

But I do what the counselor says. I agree to keep my voice down.

Questions—I got those too.

What if you're just trying to make it?

Hate without cause is a sin? What about with?

Does the fact that I did not die change my intention?

I survived—for this?

There will be no questions at this time.

No notes, ever. Just empty pill bottles left on the dresser as empty boxes of bullets. And then that one time with the straight blade, a hell of a sticky mess left behind on the bathroom floor. And then that time at the beach, doing my best Virginia Woolf. And then, most recently, on the Incurable Ward, dangling. And then, and then, and then.

That one time, the second time, is the time that should've worked. I slept for three days.

Considering the company I kept back then, it would've been a week or two before someone said, Anyone seen Rosemary? And another week before anyone did anything about it.

The poet Anne Sexton referred to it as a Lady's Death.

Snarling Donna says, Nah you gotta tie a plastic bag over your head before the pills hit, just in case.

And the counselor running the group just *lets* her.

They want to get mean. Fine, let's get mean. I was raised to be mean. Mean is a time-honored Candwell tradition. Our coat of arms might well have said, *I'll give you something to cry about!*

Shouting makes them feel strong and sure—definitely not afraid, no, perish the thought. That, or they are announcing their disregard.

Do I look like I give a fuck? says Loud-mouthed Cassie. And I consider the question as it if were really a question, scanning her for any trace of care and concern. She wriggles under my scrutiny: Quit grillin' me!

What sounds more substantial? One month, four weeks, thirty days, however many fortnights? Maybe I am on the road to Damascus.

Something we all have in common is having an opinion and its exact opposite when it is convenient. Evidence of wounds unseen. And another thing. A mood, always. A piss-poor mood, not to put too fine a point on it. It comes out of nowhere; it swallows us whole. Not sadness, something else. Something that strong-arms the sadness, telling the sadness to man up.

Forces of nature have created creatures like us. Deeply feeling creatures, somehow compelled to survive. Women bent around the shape of what we have lost, and everything reflecting our own absent form. They did it to us, they taught us how to do it, then we did it to ourselves.

I'm just so…doomed, I say.

And Snappish Cathy says, Well cry me a river, build me a bridge, and get over it. Which is pretty clever for Snappish Cathy.

I don't mean to sound bitter. I'm not bitter—not that much. But these are supposed to be my people. Why do I hate them so?

There's an insight in there. The imprint of having been raised by a woman who hates women. In fact, all iterations of my mother, every last one of her personalities and moods, are seated around this table. Maybe this idea I have, about needing to feel understood, maybe it's a fantasy. At best, a lie that tells a greater truth.

There are women who claim they are walking through the world safe and unafraid. Where are those women? Not here, that's for sure. Our own perilous lives are, to them, an adversarial menace.

What none of us ever say is, it's not fair. We know better. Someone set the record straight for us a long time ago. The person who was supposed to protect us and love us more than anything.

So when someone says, it's not fair, they are telling you everything you need to know about who they are, where they've been, what they've been taught to expect.

But I won't self-identify. It feels cheap, like it doesn't hold a candle to all that has passed. I am not a this or a that. I am not a *whatever* living with *XYZ problems*. I am a person with my own risks, my own wounds, my own responses to darkness and light.

Rosemary June Candwell is a person living and eating donuts in Pawtucket, Rhode Island. She is named after her aunt who hates her.

All rivers lead to the ocean. All cautionary tales lead back to some poison I have sewn along the way.

How can I be a victim when I have done so much?

We say survivor, the counselor says.

TAUNTED BY THE BLANK SPACE

I'm stymied by the section labeled *Skills*. Beyond my blood pressure and my old SAT score, I've got nothing left to brag about. The retooled job application of Rosemary Candwell might as well say, Give me a shot, won't you, because I'm really fucking trying.

The problem with lying on a job application is, now I have to act like I know what I'm doing. *Again*. Lies told include: I left my last job on good terms; the reference you called was definitely *not* me doing a bad Boston accent; I am a woman of my word.

Overheard at the coffee shop: A young woman says, You tell Ronnie he better be wearing a cup when he gets home tonight. An older woman on her phone, Well, the doctor called the test results a *minor setback*, if you can believe it, and someone in line ahead of me just bought the last sticky bun, so I'm kinda holding on by a thread.

And then some chin-less goateed guy in a Patriots jersey: Gimme ahh … I'm gonna get ahh…

Because it's a *coffee shop* coffee shop, a real one, with old-timers holding court in the corner every morning. A coffee shop absent an espresso machine, where we sell Keno numbers and scratch tickets, where we use Styrofoam cups, and offering breakfast sandwiches that one time nearly pushed us to the brink.

Remember that week we tried doing sandwiches? And my coworker Eileen shakes her head, looks off into the distance with a shipwrecked gaze.

But half-asleep in the morning, I can convince myself of anything. This creeping dread has its own logic. The terminal now for a terminal gal.

In the State of Rhode Island, you can no-show for three days before you are lawfully terminated. They call it job abandonment.

What's wrong with you? I say.

All I want is—what? I say.

My takeaway from that brief stint at the state-line coffee shop? I got really good at fixing toilets; the bathroom was always destroyed. But, for the life of me, I never learned what the hell the customers meant when they ordered their bagel toasted *a little on the light side*.

Finding answers in what I've lost. Finding after the fact. Go figure. It's useless, this attempt at sensibility. The idea of a solid self was just that: an idea.

I can do lots of things. I have lots of ideas. I can count on them to come apart in my hand. I can count on myself to fall to pieces.

The hulking part of me that feels broken beyond repair, it cannot be convinced there is more than this. Me, left to my own devices, without booze to blame.

Which brings me back to me being irredeemable.

What's worse, dodging your landlord isn't as cutesy as it looks in movies.

I drink a pot of coffee for breakfast and spend a good deal of time ranting about Anne Sexton.

Terminal misogyny—that's what killed her!

The shrink doesn't ask me to expand on it, but I do. I expand the hell out of it.

Her shitty male doctors were fascinated by her, so they kept her where she was. They tinkered, those motherfuckers.

And so on.

I'm sorry, I lie. I don't mean to digress. It's just that—

When did weeds get such a bum rap?

Remember in *Alice in Wonderland*? How those bitchy flowers accused Alice of being a weed? What's your genus? they said, taunting her. What's your genus? And they were horrified that she had no answer, their word for her—weed—trailing in all its judgment. What's a weed, anyway, but a plant no one planted. And isn't a weed something that grows better than what should be there?

Aftercare, aftercare, they called it aftercare at the partial hospital; the outpatient program. But after what? Time has abandoned me now that my memories are involuntary.

I tell the shrink I am regressing. I'm rereading the books of my past, my teenage years, rereading all that I've read to see what I've missed. Dressing like a camp counselor; like a small-town art teacher on a bender. Saying things like, If I have to explain, you obviously don't get it. Or rather, I imagine myself saying things like that. Is this nostalgia? I'll just do some fast math here and say, I don't know. I hate it, but I'm going with it all the same. It feels safer than being at large.

What is it that you want, Rosemary? the shrink asks, blinking, waiting.

To bear living in this world.

Meaning?

The border between myself and everything outside of myself is flimsy, basically nonexistent. What I want is to live untouched by emotion, to guide myself safely through the rest of my days. It's something to aspire to.

I used to wear impeccable eye makeup. I used to put my best face forward. What do *you* use, the customers would ask, because you look great. Now I just cry all the time. Years' worth of tears that had been locked up behind my eyes. How long had I wished for them to fall so that I might be unburdened, at last?

They never stop. Stinky onion grief. Layer after layer until I am left weeping over the sink. There's no relief though, not as I had hoped.

And everywhere I look, I see an urgent wound.

Babies, daughters, a tattered flag, a mangy street cat.

Burn, blister, broken bone—medic, medic!

What you're describing are components, the shrink says. But they're just a part of it. Like painting a picture. There isn't one stroke of the brush with which you can say, Yes, now *this* is a picture.

That's all I can tell you about, though. The parts, the mechanisms, and the what-have-you. I can tell you how these parts interact with the forces around me. But those explanations aren't as satisfying as some people would want. And by some people I mean me. Me and all my parts. We are an organism that wants to know. I can't do *what if's*. Speculation in hindsight—it's the essence of futility. What concerns me is, what now? What of it?

It's important to understand how we got here, the shrink says.

I tell her I never thought about it like that, and I am throwing her a bone. The truth is I have thought about it all the different ways. Whatever it is we are talking about.

Regarding me though? If the universe would commence bone-throwing, I sure would appreciate it.

Something in me has migrated away from reality. My secret self, emerging now that I am sequestered away from the patterns of daily life. How is it that I've come to love the aloneness? Call it Stockholm Syndrome. Call it acceptance. Resignation.

There's nobility in being alone, I lie.

My threshold is low. Like—through-the-basement low. I wouldn't mind a companion, I suppose. A Bert and Ernie bed death situation; silent mornings over coffee and toast, Early Bird Specials alight with the local news. Once you've been drained of all desire, sex and all its sexy underpinnings take on a whole new look. You see it as an alien might. Just animals, dopey and blind, seeking out friction and secretion, smashing their food holes together.

The person who says, I want to watch you watch an action movie—that's the person for me. My love of action movies is true. Their absolute rules of karmic retribution really work for me. The naysaying bastard always bites it in the end. What's not to love?

I don't want to watch this movie anymore, I had screamed aloud to no one. I pounded the remote, ham-fisted, but the DVD played on. I threw the remote at the TV, sent Dot careening into the bathroom. On-screen, a man was mauled by an attack dog, mauled to death in slow motion. Fuck *you*, I said. To the movie, the director, everyone who's had a hand in making this torture porn world we live in.

The shrink nods at everything I say, every *and then*, every *and yet*, no matter how contradictory.

I'd never hurt you.

I'm classy.

I'm a good mother.

All these things, yes, I have been told before. The things people say that indicate the very opposite of what is being said. Directly, inversely proportional. But no one ever told me, I will take care of you. And I hate myself for how much I long to hear it.

The shrink laughs and says, There's not a single person in the world who could say *I will take care of you* in any way you'd believe.

Wait, what?

What.

Help can be found, she says. But you have to believe a thing exists before you can muster the strength to look for it.

See you next week?

See you next week.

Dinner is a jar of banana peppers and five Diet Cokes. This is fine, I say, and toss the empties into the too-full blue bin.

Tension is snaking around me. A rope anchored just below my waist on my side-body, tracing the curve of my hip, then threading through my soft lower abdomen. The wheel of the world turns as a crank, pulling the rope tight, tighter, ever tighter.

I can't access the hurt. There is no range of motion in which to find comfort.

My busted-up copy of *Gray's Anatomy* tells me it's the iliacus, or maybe it's the psoas. Twin bands of muscle that form a basket for my wet insides. A quick spin online and I learn that some Buddhists call the psoas the Seat of the Soul.

A soul is a mind, and a mind is a brain in action. So basically, I'm screwed.

And what's more, a discordant pulse behind my right shoulder blade.

The women at the shelter, the long-timers, they had myriad health troubles. Chronic pain and IBS, rheumatoid arthritis and migraines. Issues in their tissues.

Life exists therefore it survives. Everything that is alive evolves.

Fuck my life, for real.

What no one talks about is how the Internet has robbed us of speculative conversation. Type, click, now you know.

Why did Robert Lowell's friends call him Cal? And how is it we landed on Peggy as a nickname for Margaret?

Let's speculate wildly! I imagine myself saying. And a spirited discussion follows. Friends seated around a kitchen table, laughing, nursing beers, absentmindedly playing some dumb card game. Penny poker, maybe. Gin Rummy.

This image lives in my memory as something imagined, but never realized. I've messed it all up. I can't make any of it happen. All of it is lost to me.

There is a cup. The cup holds twelve ounces. The cup is full. And here I am, screaming at the cup, at my mirrored face: Why can't you hold more?

Please forward my messages to the infinite void into which I am screaming.

WINTER

I COULD SLEEP
THROUGH THE COLD

That is a thing I could do.

Heavy wool socks made for men, those are my favorite. I buy them two sizes too big. For coziness, so I can feel dainty as a teacup poodle. They don't fit in my shoes, not even my snow boots. So I will stay home all winter, I guess.

I am not dainty. I come from peasant stock. Broad palms and shoulders. A spade-shaped back, strong enough to bear a lifetime of plucking root vegetables.

I am getting plumper. I'm trying to be cool with the weight gain. I am decidedly not cool with it. It's the meds, most likely. I take them without question. Or maybe I shouldn't eat donuts every time I see donuts. I do like donuts; yes, I do. Maybe I ought to take up smoking again so I can quit gummy bears. It isn't my fault they are so delicious. I will just eat less, I say. I am a cartoon woman.

The exam room is a patronizing shade of blue; insistently not pink. The nurse is a bright spot in her tie-dyed scrubs—worn ironically or sincerely, who knows, but they work. I'd tell her as much if I were in any position to pay compliments. But I am pants-less and in pain, holding my own urine.

I give the nurse my sample, tell her it's a waste of time. Every patient gets a test, she says. It's just that there's no way, not unless I'm carrying the Second Coming. The nurse doesn't laugh. Maybe she knows my kind—someone who tells a joke to practice telling the truth. Her intake questions are modest enough, but *something's wrong* is all I can manage. Family history? she asks.

On the Incurable Ward all those times before, my answer to the family question was always the same: *I am the only one.* But here in this exam room, the question holds less of a charge. Because we're talking bodies, not minds, the groovy nurse will take my word for it. My answer isn't a symptom.

I mention my mother—the mastectomy, the full hysterectomy before she was thirty . The nurse asks my age, and I answer. I make the connection only when I hear my own voice say it aloud.

They're Super Periods, I tell her. I shed all at once. It's weirdly gratifying—like when you peel an orange in a single peel. Still, she doesn't laugh.

But you felt like something was wrong, she says, enough that you came here.

I tell her how I'd dashed to the bathroom with sweat sheeting my chest and my back. *Cramping* doesn't describe it. A cramp is a charley horse or a gnarled toe turning in on itself. This was oil churning in my lower abdomen, rendering my insides, my female parts. When my heart dropped, the rest of me had followed. My shoulder clipped the sink when I went down—it spared me a greater fall.

They can't do a biopsy when you're bleeding. I would have to come back in a week. I ask if it will hurt. The groovy nurse says, No, not *hurt*. Just *cramping*.

My mother thought she was barren because she was told she was. They adopted Liz, and my mother became pregnant soon after. First with me, then Teddy. Nature was allowed to take course once the pressure was off. Her oven could function as an oven rather than a fucking vise.

Within three years of having the children she was told she'd never have, everything that made my mother anatomically female became malignant and was removed. What remained of her was flushed through with poison. She said cancer aged her. That's all she ever said about it.

At last, a daughter to spoil. Finally, a son. I think *spoil* as in ruin.

My oven is a vestigial organ I've evolved away from. When people ask me about having kids, the only way I can explain it is this: some women become mothers, some women stay daughters.

Why is it, then, that I fixate on her more than him? I'm starting to get it. The *why* of it all. She threw me to the wolf and blamed me for getting bitten.

The Home and Garden station blathers in the corner of the waiting room. I gape at the screen, expecting to be called.

A coworker told me how after her termination, she was wheeled into a recovery room with five other women. All of them, held there until someone picked them up or until someone said they were good to go. A TV was on so they'd have somewhere to look, a romantic comedy that played on a loop—the one where the heroine is career-driven (read: sexless and cold) and suffers a string of humiliations en route to having it all.

The rom-com, the Home and Garden station, the *not pink* walls: These were all decisions. Someone thought these decisions made sense. My coworker said she watched the movie twice without realizing.

I'm left in the exam room long enough to imagine leaving. I know how this sounds, I'd tell them, but I really think I'm okay.

The doctor enters at a clip. She would do two passes. She calls them passes. Scoot down to the edge of the table, scoot more, more. Knees forced apart, penetrated with something unknowable.

So I freeze. I'm punctured and I freeze. I'm frozen but I can still feel the feeling, I think I can. A murky image viewed from above, a small body beneath me, a girl's body, my body, frozen and dead and punctured.

Stop, my voice says. The doctor looks up. I apologize. She says don't apologize. I apologize for apologizing; I try to explain.

What happened to me remained in my viscera, even when the rest of me forgot. The body remembers, is what my shrink says. But everything's come back and my mind's come undone and I guess I'm just like this now.

The doctor does a good impression of understanding.

One pass will have to be enough; I cannot do another. She says I can. I can and I should. But I am firm, and she can tell.

The doctor snaps off her gloves and turns on her heel. The squeak of her clog fills the room. No news is good news, she says with a huff. If I don't hear back, then my results are clear. The door opens and closes. I lay still, crying, until her squeaking steps fade.

Two weeks go by without a word. I call; I ask what's the deal. The voice on the other end is curt: No news is good news, didn't they tell you?

But I still think something is wrong.

This just happens as you get older. You're just like this now.

The voice keeps going, but nothing registers. Crossing over, departing from sleep. In these first moments of waking, I realize how deeply I've been under. Ocean metaphor, cave metaphor, blah, blah, blah. All I know is, I've awoken in a nightmare. Nothing is as it seems.

I'm just like this now.

THEY'RE COMING AND GOING

It's a nonstop turnaround in this building, sullen art students and grad students handing off their studios like slumming is a credit to earn. It seems to be, me and Geronimo are the only ones who really live here.

His daughter's eyes are red-rimmed and wild, peering into the space my door chain allows. I hold the knob tight, pull the door flush against my cheek. I tell her, No, I haven't seen him, just his car parked out front.

She's been trying him for days, she says, and thought it best to come by. But his car … with all the snow.

I saw as much when I left for work earlier. Geronimo's old Mercury looks like a three-room igloo, still plowed in deep from the blizzard. I figured he tied one on during the storm, blacked out, and slept it off.

I ask if she's got a key, tell her to let herself in. She draws a staggered breath, wincing to keep her tears in place. She thought she had a key but can't find it anywhere. Her tears unlock with *anywhere*.

I close the door and release the chain, step into the hall and shut the door behind me. I offer to call the landlord—he'll help her out. Except he's a drunk like Geronimo's a drunk. If he can peel away from the barstool, if he can drag himself out of whatever dive he's propped up in, sure, he'll help her out. Bastard sends me to voicemail. My message is straight and serious: Call back right away when you get this.

I offer to write down his number; tell her to keep trying. Her chin falls to her chest. She rounds in defeat.

My eyes scan the hallway like the solution is in the baseboard heating or thick-peeling paint. We'll call the police, then. She finds my eyes at the sound of we.

I punch in the numbers and clear my throat. Hearing the bit about Geronimo's car parked out front, buried under feet of snow, the voice on the other end cuts me off. They'll send someone over right away.

I sit on the stairs by my apartment door and pat the spot beside me. She lowers herself down tautly. Some cedary aroma issues from her scarf with every nervous shudder. I introduce myself, and she says, I'm Sylvie? Like she's not even sure.

I scan her for something suspect. Sylvie is a walking, talking Tarot card. She'd look right as rain with a sword at her hip and a snake around her neck, wearing leather and velvet in all seasons. Her hair is bruise-colored, wound up in a high topknot. And she's got a picked and peeled anxiety manicure, same as me. Tiny red islands floating above her fingernail moons. I recognize her coat—a breathtaking '80s cocoon. It had been prominently displayed in the consignment store window around the time I first got hired.

Did I ring her up? Unlock a fitting room? Was I kind? I hope so but I know I wasn't. The store, the students, the whole deal—I've gone sour. Sourer.

The squabble of walkie-talkies announces their arrival. I feel obliged to do the talking as the one who made the call. I greet them awkwardly, introducing Sylvie with a flourish like we're at a cocktail party.

No one has to tell me to leave. I leave them to it, the grim task at hand.

My father is dead. Or so I've said to anyone who's ever bothered to ask. Another lie that tells a greater truth.

He had called twice when I was in the shelter; left me rambling messages. Peaks and valleys, he'd said, telling me he understood, never offering to help. His words were damp with cheap booze I could smell through the phone. Over and over he said life is just peaks and valleys. When he told me he was worried, I never once believed that it was me he was worried about.

It took time, saving up. I called my parents after I moved in, even my brother and sister. Told them I got a job, a place of my own. I could demonstrate *I am better now*—did they want to come by?

My father was the only one who showed. He prowled the two rooms, circling and scanning. His stomping feet filled the near-empty space and gave him false authority. Where's the rest of your stuff? he wanted to know.

And I—

My father looked into my face. An absent moment of remembering, not the fire, but what the fire burned.

I held his gaze until he balked.

He said he had an appointment, made a line for the door.

What happens in this house stays in this house. His left eye twitches when he says it. A tic. A tell. We are his slabs of marble, beaten and ground and chiseled away. He doesn't care if the hammer falters, crumbling us to dust.

One night he overdoes it. It marks an *ending*, of sorts. The only thing we all agree on is that we all were there. Everything else is suited to mind, even the police report.

Broken bones don't leave a mark. My body remembers that night when it rains.

I tune my ears to the floor above, beyond my booming pulse. The squawk of walkie-talkies, lost in its blare. Then it's Sylvie. Crying out with disbelief. And something else—something unknowable until you know it, just like grief itself.

The walkie-talkies grow louder. The leaden footsteps of blue uniforms make their way down the stairs by my door. I hold my breath as they pass.

I open my phone to call someone. *Anyone.* To tell them what has happened, to reach beyond what I've come to expect. Supposing care and concern as opposed to the usual nothing. I look into the gray screen until it dims.

Another knock, a teeny knock made by the tiniest fist. She's faint and shrunken inward, a picture of dashed hope.

I motion to the kitchen table. I take a seat by her side.

Our hands match. Withered from cold, gnawed to the quick, laid flat on the table before us. Tiny red islands floating above our fingernail moons.

I hear my heart beating. It keeps time with the plastic clock above the door. I hear her heart beating. Seconds tick by.

Tiny red islands. Little white moons.

NEVER HAVE I EVER BEEN

The one who leaves, the one who walks out. And yet—
It's called an evolutionary imperative.

All of January takes on the look of a dream.
I am in Carcosa now. Song of my soul, my voice is dead.
No need to segue.

Liz is a record that skips. She favors invented nostalgia. Teddy is a redacted document. He never looks back. Effective strategies, it's true. But I am the warehouse. I am the one who remembers.

We have always been pitted against one another; we were raised to be at odds. Childhood games that ended with trips to the emergency room. How one time, a hotly contested round of Jenga culminated with punches thrown, all of us whipping wooden blocks, and Teddy had to wear an eye patch for two weeks.

The last time I saw them all together I did not know it was the last time. What would I have said had I known? Probably nothing, as is my way.

I say together like we were all bound as one, but that's not how it was. What were we, then, if not bound as a single unit? Who's to say.

We were only our own thing; our own slow-rotting thing.

They all wore a look of surprise Christmas morning. A sharp suspended silence as I came through the door, interrupting their conversation. My parent's house—my father's house—with doors that had on numerous occasions been opened wide to both my brother and sister. Opened to their entire families—Liz's two kids and husband, Teddy's wife and their yipping dog.

Well, yes, I was invited. I told you I would be here, so here I am.

They thought I would be out cavorting and carousing. That, or all alone. Holding one idea and its opposite as a single fact.

In the past, I would have shaken off their surprise, continued showing up, hat in hand, mewling and submissive. My hair shirt, all laid out and waiting for me. But on the bus ride home, as the 36 rattled up Beverage Hill, as the Christmas sun deadened around me, my face appeared in the window against the mauve of wintry twilight. Me as I was and me as I came to be, rolling in and out of frame. For a moment, all moments, as the past became real. The effect was total.

You're smarter than them, I said to my reflection. But remember when you fought for your life though? Where did that come from?

I pulled the string overhead, stumbled to the front of the bus. This is where I get off.

Pattern recognition is the keystone evolutionary trait in the human animal. I am part of a larger pattern. I am the first witness, unlikely to produce any more.

You're not acting like yourself, Teddy had told me Christmas morning.

How am I not myself?

I started with him because I thought he would understand. I thought he would say, Don't I know it. But all Teddy said was, You can't prove it.

How the human mind can pull out a blindfold. That's the connection—the unspoken contract between a whole long line of us, spanning back in time.

Can't prove it.

When you hear a grown man say, My father taught me how to be strong. … Girl, *run*, don't walk.

There was a deeper, sadder side to all that we withstood. I'm talking about the sense within my father that we were not his children. We were his adversaries, a force loose in his own house meant to mirror back at him all he'd lost along the way.

Hurt people hurt people, they say.

Except, fuck that.

I imagine him thick-tongued and slurring. That was a tough time for all of us, he might say. But only when he's a few beers deep.

He's tried to get the grandkids to call him Papa. My sister Liz has played along. Where's your hug for Papa? And those sweet kids shrink small enough to disappear right off the Earth. Kids know, they say. Kids and dogs.

The idea of roping in another generation—that's what did it.

I suppose I should tell you what's been going on with me, I said. Because of the kids; her kids.

All that happened, and all that has happened since, was positioned for Liz as a cautionary tale. I laid out how I got here to keep them from becoming like me. It wasn't a strategy, not really, just a means to be heard.

You're not *listening*, I said, crying. I tried to stop and only made it worse. Crying, I knew, undid my argument.

Liz came out hot. When did you become such a lying scumbag, Rosemary?

I said, I'm not sure, as if I had often wondered the same thing. My sister wishes I were different and I wish I were different too.

One-way doors everywhere—how I came to realize I could never see Liz again. Her children, like lambs to the slaughter. So she can, what? Prove a point?

And lastly, my mother. She said she didn't know what to say, as if saying so were enough.

He confiscated something from me. But to you, what was taken was not taken. It had been forfeited. I got what I deserved.

This is what I should have said, but didn't.

In the end, what I told her was, she could never again say that she never knew.

When she hung up, it was the dial-tone-less hang up of a cell phone, without so much as a click. Just silence, the sense of deletion. Whatever had been there, gone. Fitting, really. Nothing open-ended about it.

What have I left behind? The tightly woven silence of adults bound together, reasserting their version of the truth.

No, what really happened was…

But they do not breathe a word.

I say *left*. I say *broke away*. Yet that implies an unwilling party, someone on the other side saying, Please don't go.

It's just Crazy Rosemary being crazy again. … And I made it easy, didn't I? With every committal, every emergency room and elopement risk warning. With my arms opened wide, my body dangling, my guts wrung out. And that one time I tried to drown, but couldn't.

If this then that. Made, not born. Nothing exists in a vacuum. No one.

I broke the rule when first I spoke. I took what happened in that house out of the house. Laid it all on the table, words no longer minced.

This—*this* is what's wrong, what has always been wrong. Most of me, if not all of me, aligned at last to say, *Enough.*

Is it in me to contemplate gone? Is it in anyone?

Attachment, yes.

Tethered and falling. Falling while tethered.

Dread, yes.

This is family as I have known it.

The stain will linger. There are times when it can be hidden away, hidden even from myself. But then it reappears and, in reappearing, appears to spread. Up my throat, across my face.

Other scars too. There's not enough vitamin E in the world. All those razors drawn, cigarettes extinguished. When I am very hot or when I am very cold, they raise up on my forearms. Angry violet streaks and dots, constellations that form shapes but no pictures. Exploding fucking stars.

It's like this because it has always been like this.

Poisoned groundwater. Fruit of a poisoned tree.

Made, not born. All of us.

This is where I get off.

IF YOU HAD TOLD ME
IT WOULD BE THIS WAY

I would've said you ought to stop huffing glue. But this is a little like huffing glue, isn't it? Because I think what's happened is, I've had a lapse. Like when you put the milk in the cupboard and the cereal in the fridge.

I was sluggish and tired, so I drank a pot of coffee. Now I am sluggish and tired and brutally aware of how sluggish and tired I am.

You'd do well to stay away from coffee, my shrink says.

I think, From my cold dead heads. Think, but do not say. For once, not.

I saw Fourth of July fireworks in the sky above Mount Washington when I was eight. The fireworks were well and good—I was eight, they were fireworks. But it's the sound of them I remember most, an endless call and response between the peaks of the Presidential Range.

Would you say that's a fond memory? my shrink asks.

More of an artful transition.

What I want to talk about is acoustic shadow. How it played a major role in the Civil War, when the *sound* of a battle was the quickest way a commander could judge the *course* of a battle. The closer they were, the less they could hear. Decisions were made accordingly.

That's quite an analogy, my shrink says.

It's not an analogy, just fascinating is all. Bloody battles—deadlier, more brutal in blunt force than modern wars. They were shaped and altered by snowfall, or a strong wind blowing from north to south. Sounds were absorbed, refracted, or just blown in a different direction. Like Stonewall Jackson's attack against the Union Army on the banks of the Potomac. It was bold—reckless, even. So it's easy to assume the attack only worked because an acoustic shadow gave them cover.

But assumptions are suited to mind, my shrink says. Especially in hindsight.

What I wonder is, did the soldiers blame themselves? Like they had somehow dropped the ball? Because it's easier to redirect blame than it is to subscribe to some freaky kind of phenomenon, the kind that doesn't make sense.

Like repressed memories, like a person forgetting the worst things that happened to them—that makes no sense at all.

I mean, you hear a bomb blast because it's loud and deadly. You hear a bomb blast and you take cover. Right?

When we were kids, my sister threatened to call the authorities. My father would hand her the phone: Do it. I'll dial.

You've never mentioned that before, my shrink says.

Except Liz never got it like me and Teddy did. Maybe because she was adopted, like she was some precious gift, maybe my father thought that would be *wrong*. Still, she was terrorized all the same.

Once the War was over, everyone wanted to forget just how bloody, how brutal, how avoidable it all was. But some things can't move towards healing. A bone, broken, that sets incorrectly has to be broken again so it can truly mend.

She slapped her three-year-old in front of us on Christmas morning, full-handed. I gasped. Teddy reddened and stormed out of the room. My father shook his head. Not on the face, Liz, not where it leaves a mark. That's what he said.

The sound of that slap, the pitch of persecution in my sister's voice as she wagged her finger in that sweet boy's face—it broke something in me. Some fixed way of being cracked right down the center.

One in three were dead, gone, or wounded after the battle at Gettysburg. Among those marked safe on the other side of the fight, who could've let the one in three pass without mourning? And how could the sun have risen over Gettysburg? It rises, still.

Heat was a factor. Heat hot as static, hot as white noise. It swallowed up the sounds of war on the ground.

The heat had surprised me. How hot it could be when there was nowhere to hide. My nook was tucked below the sidewalk on Pine Street, beneath the stairway leading to an Indian restaurant. The noise above my head would pull me from sleep. Street sweepers and garbage trucks, road construction and utility work with no rhyme or reason, just a fevered pace to *get it done*, whatever it was.

Bright and early, and downtown would smell of low tide. A smoldering sunrise indicated an Air Quality Alert Day. If the sky was a fiery haze, I could ride the bus for free.

The only people who rode to beat the heat were street people, people like me. We all took the longest routes, from Providence to Newport, from Providence to Woonsocket, all day long. My ruminations kept me company. Thoughts like, why does the English language have only a single word for grief? Also, if I recognized the faces of other street people riding the bus, did that mean they recognized me?

Then someone says, Maybe it'll burn off. Some old-timer across the aisle. He means the humidity. Maybe the sun will crackle hot and dry enough to cut through the soupy air. I peel my eyes from the window; tell him I'm sorry, I'm not in the mood to talk to anyone. His face is full and hollow. He wilts at the sound of my voice. This Old Bitch seated behind me calls me a Little Bitch. Tells me to quit acting like my shit don't stink—like I'm not riding the bus like the rest of them.

I once told my mother I hated her. I hate you with the fire of a thousand suns, is what I said. She called me a Little Bitch and said she hated me too.

That's the thing. Silence led to inaction. I imagine the commanders were ashamed to admit they'd been deaf to the fighting. After the fact, after the smoke cleared and the casualties were counted, all eyes turned to the one in charge demanding to know, what happened?

I can't stop reading about it.

Well, your way bends toward *understanding*, my shrink says. Minds assign meaning. The meaning isn't inherently there.

I've been looking for myself in all that I've read ever since I was a girl. When all I knew was how I felt and how I felt made no sense. What I felt daily and every night.

My shrink reminds me I've done the right thing, getting away from them—all of them. She says, Repeat after me: *I did not deserve it.*

I talk about my mother more than my father. He cracked me wide open and told me I was the reason why. But my mother finished the job.

Expand on that, my shrink says.

I'm never far from the girl I was, though I scarcely remember that girl was me. That girl needed a mother. The grief I feel is for someone that never existed.

And then it's too late. I am crying an ugly cry. The voice that ekes out of me is a thin wisp of a voice. I cannot hear all that I say.

Indifference is the goal here. But I dwell in the memory of my memories, or how it was that all was forgotten. How unconsciousness was a gift.

What I do is, I eat starchy foods to weigh myself down, to thicken the grooves of my mind and keep the rattle to a dull roar.

Sleepy foods, long dark nights. Still, a phantom paces behind my eyes.

The heavy foods don't work. They've turned me plump and dumb. A walking potato.

But now I get it, the appeal of monastic living.

You catch a glimpse of something. The glimpse reorders all of you. You have no choice. You get the hell out of Dodge.

Twenty-eight days filled with snow that's not fluff. Gray ice melding with an endlessly gray sky. Weather that hurts my face. I live in a place with weather that hurts my face.

I can barely hear him through the barroom din in the background, my landlord all gummed up with rot-gut whiskey. He tells me he's glad I called, that he's been meaning to stop by.

The way you *handled* the whole Gerry situation—

Gerry?

Geronimo.

Not sure what it is I *handled*.

Still, he says. Thank you.

There's that thing in middle-aged men, the flickering presence of mortality when a massive coronary takes one of their own.

Do you have—*a bird*?

It's my cat, I tell him. She's in heat.

You should really get her fixed, my landlord slurs. It's irresponsible not to.

So, the hot water will be back on when?

I know you did the best you could do, is a thing they like to say. In movies and TV shows and greeting cards. *They* don't know what the fuck they're talking about.

SPRING

TELL A STORY, HAVE SOME THOUGHTS ABOUT IT

That's what these appointments are. Telling a story, having some thoughts about it. Thumbing the beads of an abacus because it is positioned precisely at thumbing distance, set on a small end table to my right.

I ask her why, like a child. But what I really mean is *how*.

The sky is blue—how?

I am an orphan—how?

It hurts—how?

Properties of awakening uncongenial to me, with my stupid brain eager to ask questions. Questions with no answers and so they will be asked forever. I claim to seek a purpose, but what I really seek is an explanation of precedence.

I've been taken back the long way, the hard way. I have crossed some unmarked border. It had looked the same; scenery unchanged. Until I found myself looking down the muzzle of a rifle, a foreign voice, angry and questioning, and my only answer: I don't know, I don't understand!

At first it was scary, the steady loss of myself. How the losing never stopped and there was nothing to be done about it.

What can be said about the systematic destruction of reality? Once I pulled the thread it was revealed to me that I never really existed. An origin story, a sense of identity that amounts to nothing more than a failure of imagination. The remote soul of a woman structured around guilt and shame and silence and blame. In kind, a depression has taken hold, but one cosmic and existential. Which is new.

Or not. I don't know, it's hard to explain. I am tired of explaining. I am tired of trying to explain. Mixed metaphors abound here on the other side of whatever the hell, and for what? My only tools are warped and weird, mostly ineffective, and always, always misinterpreted by others.

Put me back down. I wish to go back to sleep.

My shrink says, When you're despairing like this, when you can't find the words, it's likely the youngest parts of you, drawn to the surface at last.

And I gasp, Yeah, but … I just want. … All I want is …

My shrink has a name, and that name is Elle. How she could be my mother, age-wise—this is not lost on me. A cliché, yes, but no less accurate for being a cliché. Yet Elle is not scornful of me, and she does not condescend. So, no, not a Mother Figure. More like a port in the storm.

Elle invites me into the possible future. In this possible future I can be anything.

A plant person, with high white walls and sun-soaked rooms dripping green life.

A soulful yoga person, a plant-eater, lithe and de-boned and eager to hug a stranger.

An art person, ironic and deliberate, cultivating eccentricities.

A career person, with a planner and a vision board and a concrete sense of actionable goals achieved over time.

A mothering person; with children, yes, but with coworkers and foster pets and scores of friends, too, all gathered around the table in a farmhouse-style kitchen, because mothering people have great soup recipes and can remember if it's *feed a cold, starve a fever*, or whether it's the other way around.

These are the survivor archetypes, feminized models of some great purpose-driven *after*, none of which have a Rosemary-shaped shape to them. Because how could they?

Call it muscle memory. A special kind of doubt I reserve only for myself. No version of me will be spared.

Where can you soften? Elle asks. Reject nothing.

There were no ties to the past in that house growing up. No photo albums or scrapbooks, no family traditions or recipes that threaded the generations together. A blue-collar household as an American midcentury household, forever and ever. But miserable. So, so miserable.

The only photos were our school portraits; me, Liz, and Teddy staggered on the staircase wall in ascending order by age, switched out with each passing year and, once removed, never to be seen again. The terminal present.

I did not know what I was looking at. She was seated alone at the kitchen table, rounded over the school portraits laid out before her. Inky blue dusk filled the window over the sink, the twenty or so minutes of quickening November nightfall when the day is done but the lights haven't been turned on yet. My eyes adjusted and the context was revealed. How she had hidden away the photos in plain sight, kept them bound together in the frames, kept only for her, and viewed once a year. I had caught her in the act, taking in the look of time. Her arms rung around the faces of her children, as we were and as we came to be, gathering us up, hoarding what little remained.

Or protecting? Elle asks.

I laugh a bitter laugh. It crackles in the small space of her office, in the distance between us, seated across from one another, knee to knee.

I'm sorry, it's just. … What I'm trying to say is, soft as she appeared, she was a stranger to me. It's important you know what I mean.

No, I know what you mean, Elle says. And she does.

Je-sus, Mary, and Joseph! You scared me half to death, my mother had said, quickly collecting the photos, summoning her indignation. No one likes a sneak, Rosemary June! You, sneaking around in the dark.

And what I said to her was—

Really, it doesn't matter, does it? My mother called it backtalk and she wanted none of it, *not under this roof.*

The reverence for capital-F family is something I keep coming up against. How people can't handle the defilement of what they've presumed to be the natural order.

Elle asks, Is there something she could have said that would have been enough? When you told her how it was?

I love you, maybe. Or, I'm glad you've told me. I know you didn't choose this. … That would've fixed everything.

A family pact made of silence so that things might carry on, so that the house wouldn't come crashing down. And now, like an angry mob, like a civil jury, they insist their greater number reveals a greater truth. Or something.

If I had the money, I would raze that fucking house on Roscoe Avenue. Then I'd torch the rubble. I'd burn it to cinder, render it to dust.

At every crossroads, in an effort to keep one foot in front of the other, the youngest, most wounded parts of me were forced deep beneath the surface.

But all that I submerged has risen, returning to me like a poorly weighted corpse. Corpses, as in many. The unwilling, salvaged dead. The versions of myself that have been throttled in the dark.

We don't say *commit*, Elle says. We say *died by*. The former implies the act of suicide is a sin, when really it is just an implemented strategy.

Elle can be so matter-of-fact when she wants to be.

And what about him? Elle says. What would it look like if you had the chance to confront him, as you are now?

I would fight him. I would beat him bloody. I would stand over his beaten body and delight in his look of fear.

Because?

Because. That's as close to time travel as I will ever get. Violent retribution as time travel.

The neighbors who heard screaming children, stomping boots, and crashing doors. The neighbors who drew their blinds to spinning red and blue lights; who whispered, That's none of our business; who ventured, There must be two sides to this story … I get their friend requests on social media.

I rough away the sweat sheen on my forehead and my upper lip. Anger, all the time and out of nowhere. Sweating and cursing and crying and sweating. God bless a black tank top. A black t-shirt. And panty liners as pit pads, although that never really works as well as I'd like.

Elle says, If you stop and listen, you can hear what the anger has to say. What is it telling you?

That something has been broken. Something has to be rebuilt.

But remembering, the fallout of remembering, means I now move through the world feeling as though I am scorched to the bone.

You're resilient, she adds. You have burned so that you might emerge.

I am cursed, is what I am.

Elle's kindness—the birthday card she has handed me, the birthday card she bought with money, and inscribed with something heartfelt. It knocks the air from my lungs.

Stop trying to get me to cry, I scream, crying. I have to take two buses to get home after this. Two!

I leave the chair, leave the room then the office. I pace the sidewalk, think up my scenarios, my angry confrontations, and keep them to myself. I board the bus—one of the two—and ride off, gazing out the rain-streaked window as if I were in a music video. A 1980's power ballad with smash-cut slow-mo footage of the band's life on the road.

I cannot escape being their daughter any more than I can escape the many-faceted dimensions of my shattered fucking mind. Ain't that the way.

It's just a matter of time before the face I see in the mirror becomes her face; and my hands, her hands. Odd bits and parts too. Her meaty knees. The rounded defeat in her cervical spine.

This me of the possible future, whoever she is, she will not color her hair as the white comes in. She will let it go. She will see what happens next. White, not gray. As with my mother. Both grandmothers. Their mothers too, I assume.

For some reason I cannot account for, I turn calm. Not peaceful, no, just impassive.

A reminder: Not being a piece of shit is still an option that's available to you, Rosemary. I will text Elle an apology. Not now, but soon. Soon enough.

ALL BABIES
ARE NOT BEAUTIFUL

But this baby? This baby is cute as hell. And I mean it! But I guess I'm the asshole here, judging from how quickly the young mother gets up and changes her seat on the bus.

One thing that might rattle my ovaries? Tiny fingernails the size of a caper. They extend my capacity to stand in mystery. How even the worst of us were ever that small. But there's a metaphor in there somewhere. The caper-sized fingernails cut like a razor. Catch it at the right angle, and the caper will cut you to ribbons.

What I like about kids, though, is they're straight shooters. The boy in the diner, hands cupped over his ears, screaming, It's too loud in here! The girl in CVS, splayed on the floor, skirt up, Pampers out, crying, I don't wanna do it anymore! They are acting out their inner world.

Their mothers might mean mug me, but still I salute them in solidarity. Go forth, kid. Stick it to the man.

Except children are squishy little sponges with no one to wring them out over the sink. What keeps baby fever in check—if that's what this is. The planet is dying.

ℰ

Another day, another step closer to full-tilt misandry. In Kennedy Plaza, two damp-eyed crust punks compare staph infections.

A flier is thrust into my hand. The school portrait of a twelve-year-old girl with a shiny bright Say Cheese! smile but unmistakably sad eyes. A runaway from New Hampshire, thought to be on her way to Providence. A girl with a plan.

When I ran away at ten, I had packed a small bag and took off in a hurry. Had no idea where I was headed but made sure to bring my bathing suit with me because you never know.

One grown up. One adult that could see me, could glean what was happening without me having to say a word. All I ever wanted. So this urge to volunteer is rooted in a question: Who is it that I needed when I was young?

Icebreaker is just another word for a getting-to-know-you exercise: Name a fact that few people would know about you.

I tell the group I very well may have swallowed every piece of gum I've ever had. Gentle laughter rumbles throughout the seated circle. No, I'm being serious. One time I ate an entire pack of Big Red when I was super stoned. I couldn't help it; I was just so snacky. And then there's only a single voice laughing. A husky, smoky laugh, one strangely familiar.

The world is coming for all these dirtbag men, or so the world says. The Helpline training is packed. These are women with their fists in the air, and good for them. People need to believe in adversity overcome.

The only way out is through. The only way out is through. Except here I am, cornered by around people; the prescriptive type. They want so badly to convince me they have the answers; they have arrived! Like the long-lost women who reach out to me through the window of social media. Former classmates trying to on-board me to whatever pyramid scheme they've bought into. Stop calling it a journey, Caitlin, you're selling protein shakes.

Working at the Helpline requires six whole days of training. Here we are, day one of six, and already there's so much talk of good vibes. But I don't want their good vibes, keep 'em offa me!

It's a world of grad student nonsense. Those well-meaning types, regurgitating something they learned in a workshop. All theory, no application. Virtue never tested, and whatnot. Ride a city bus for a week and then get back to me, is definitely something I do not say out loud.

If I sound judgmental it's because I am. Some people are capable of surprising me. Not these people, though.

They want me to share my sad stories. They call it space making. I call it fuck you very much.

Still I do it, I do the thing. I set myself on fire to be a light for another. One of them calls me inspirational and I grow smaller.

A booming signal from within. Blood percussive in my ears. My viscera contract to a point. At the center, a red-faced malcontent roils with news of certain destruction edging closer, closer.

I excuse myself. I find a bathroom. I take cover.

A wave of inner revolt. A pull in my chest, my left shoulder deadens, a gone-to-sleep tingle then all of my left hand goes numb. Truncated breaths, crackling sweat. I am brought to my knees.

I hold onto the bathroom floor. I hold my insides in. I hold on.

We have been here before, we have always been here. We will not panic at this panic attack. We will let the train barrel through the station.

How I'm always saying, Hell is not a place you go; it's something you carry around inside you. Like that.

I am drawn back into my body, propped up against the wall. Somewhere between a memory and a mirage, counting tiles beneath the heels of my hands. The obvious *lavatory* smell—cheap brown paper towels, powdered bleach—but cut with an earthen aroma entirely out of place. She's seated beside me, her cedary fragrance coming off of her in waves.

Sylvie. The walking, talking Tarot card; the single voice laughing, her husky, smoky laugh. Geronimo's daughter, suffusing light and warmth on this basement bathroom floor.

Been awhile, she says, smiling.

The din of the Helpline training session drones on above our heads; the clapping, the surge of woo-hooing. Sounds like this thing is wrapping up, she says. I nod, nodding too fast, like a dolt. Wanna come over? Catch up?

I say yes without hesitation. Of course I say yes.

Aloneness is impossible to shake. I have tried. I have come up short. I had long known the feeling, the full and hollow feeling. But when I came to among beeps and drips—stitched-up, wanting my mother, needing my mother, waiting for her, knowing she would never come—I named and claimed aloneness as my lot in life, once and for all. These days? What can I say, I really lean into it.

I've told Elle, I have no friends because people don't like to feel ineffective.

How so?

Because I am an immovable, un-climbable mountain.

I've had work friends, yes, proximity friends. I do well with proximity friendship.

Maybe things would be different if I drove, if I had a car. I'd gladly pick up a friend at the airport. I'd be happy to help a friend move.

I'm no innocent here. I am not given up on. I get ahead of the game and give up on others. My parts insist I never lower the drawbridge for anyone. And yet—

After the Geronimo ordeal, after we sat together, awaiting the coroner, silently drinking glass after glass of cloudy tap water, me and

Sylvie had awkwardly exchanged numbers, but only in a wrap-it-up sort of way.

My phone is turned off at the moment, she'd murmured.

But, you know … just in case, I had said.

Yeah, just in case. She was glazed with grief but somehow managed a smile. I was touched that she was touched.

The walk to Sylvie's place is short, but long enough for me to consider all the ways I could bail, should bail, ought to. Oh man, I totally forgot I have to…

She is seamless, though, going on about the training; how the team-building stuff is dippy, for sure, but she can't wait to get actual work done at the Helpline. Because of the atrocious way women have been treated lately, she says, and all the years leading up to lately.

Her last attempt at volunteering didn't go so great. To be fair, she says, they told me a million times that clinic escorts shouldn't engage the protesters. But I had no choice, not after I'd memorized all those Bible verses. I mean, c'mon, someone's gotta stick it to those old, crusty motherfuckers, harassing young women.

She tells me she went with The Sermon on the Mount: It says *as the hypocrites do*, and I'd hit *hypocrites* hard just to see those bastards flinch.

I bet she was popular with the patients—of course she was. Who among us wouldn't want an enforcer; someone to push back, harder.

That's so rad, I say and I apologize. Can't pull off rad; never could. How did you know it would do the trick, The Sermon on the Mount?

She pauses, gives the empty street a sidelong look-see. My mother and stepfather are pretty Christian, she whispers.

How Christian?

Well—they say the Lord. A lot.

Her place is lined with books, beautiful books with cloth-covered bindings. They still the full volume of the space. I've hauled them around for years, she says, but I'm thinking of cutting them loose, going minimal, travelling light. Lately I've been into books on tape. Something about being read to, she says, trailing off dreamily in a way that doesn't make me want to scoff. Somehow, doesn't.

Without consultation, Sylvie puts on *Pet Sounds*, plops onto a floor cushion, deftly rolls a spliff of dank weed sprinkled with red hairy tobacco. She sparks it efficiently, offers it to me with an easy smile. I take a slow drag, welcoming the familiar burn pulling my chest apart. Been awhile, indeed.

You ever think about how The Ramones are basically The Beach Boys in leather jackets?

And yes, yes I've had that exact thought a hundred times. But I am stoned, too stoned, hard and fast and feeling odd, so the words won't form in my mouth.

She cranks the volume; lays on the carpet, arms and legs stretched as star points. And she listens, her face bathed in the most peaceful expression.

Try as I might, I cannot hear it as she hears it. I avert my eyes, I close my eyes, I sit up straight, I lounge back on the couch. But the layered harmonies fill the room as the din in a crowded bar, pushed back, pushed away. I hear only my own voice in my head. My parts speaking to me from across the table. They go on and on, listing their reasons, making their case. Their case is strong: no good days, not for you.

Did you know there was a special section at Grateful Dead shows for hearing impaired fans? They'd hold balloons, she says, held close to their chests, to feel the music as vibrations beneath their fingertips. She takes a deep pull of the joint. The cherry illuminates her face like she's telling a ghost story. That's all sound is, she says, croaking through a held drag: *Vibrations*.

Never would've pegged you for a Deadhead, I say.

No way, she says. Deadheads give the Dead a bum rap.

But you're into jam bands and the like?

First of all, ew, no. Second, *how dare you?* She laughs, tosses her head back, revealing the long line of her throat.

Far be it from me to yuck your yum. I would *never*.

Her laugh. Her throat.

I keep my favorites to myself, I tell her.

Not me, she says. I wanna scream from the mountain tops whenever I discover something that moves me.

I'm not a recommender. I covet.

You must be a middle child, she says, smiling, lolling on the carpet, stretching like a cat.

Sylvie's skin is a work of art. *Mostly.* She rolls her sleeve up high, revealing the lingering trace of a blurry blue-black tribal armband around her bicep. From when I was young and dumb, she says. I won't cover it up though. I'm happy to have a permanent reminder of just how idiotic I can be when left to my own devices.

I'm only an apprentice, she says sheepishly. I picture her hammering iron, wearing a tricorne hat. Really, apprenticeship entails answering the phone, making appointments, cleaning up shop, and in between, tattooing melons and sometimes herself. So far, she says, my biggest contribution to that place is the sign I painted above the piercing station in the corner. It says: There is no body part called the click. Exclamation point.

She used to be a yoga teacher, she tells me, but hung it up after Geronimo died. I hate myself for being a cliché, she says, but stupid yoga really helped me. For a while, teaching had the look of a solution.

Fledgling students would hug her tightly. Others could smell their own; a survivor in their midst. They told her to stay strong—older women, brimming with white-hot anger. How she knew she was done for good: She told the class, If you're looking to be happy all the time there's the door. And three people got up and left. *Three.*

Worshipping the teapot instead of drinking the damn tea, I say. Sylvie's eyes stretch and widen like I've handed her a gold bar.

She's proud of her hot, firm ass; stands up and presents it to me, and I confirm, yes, it is truly hot and firm. She's into power lifting;

hoisting and schlepping. She calls it empowering. It's an all-women gym, she says. You ought to come with me.

A blasted alarm, a call from within me to pick up the slack: Why, when I'm already carrying the full weight of my existential dread?

She draws herself up to meet my eye. Who took your joy, Rosemary? This from the woman who discovered her father dropped dead on his kitchen floor four months ago.

All I'm saying is, don't you want it back? She blinks sluggishly, and waits for me to do the explaining.

I cannot produce anything like an answer. There's no epiphany in sight. So what I do is, I bare my seams. I speak of monsters and mirrors and secrets given up slowly.

A lightly held silence, then Sylvie says: On your—on your birthday? There was a neat math to it—it was compelling.

What you should do is, you should reorient. Celebrate your half-birthday in September. Reclaim your solar return!

That's your takeaway?

How best to describe this creature seated before me: she believes in Mercury Retrograde but not hand sanitizer.

My shrink speaks often about my pre-traumatized self, as if it is an actual person alive out there in the world. And every time I tell her, frankly, I have no idea who that could be. Because it's not like we're unpacking a single incident. There wasn't one cataclysmic event that forever divided time into then and now, before and after. Who I was is no one I could ever get to know.

Try, Sylvie says. Just try to imagine her, even if it's only a story.

A child, a reader. A daydreamer, yes, but more of an observer than an inventor. She loved the mountains before she ever laid eyes on them, and felt rightfully at ease in the ocean. She read of a place where the mountains meet the sea and thought that it very well may be possible there is a place on Earth made just for her.

How old? Sylvie says.

Hard to say. How old are you in kindergarten? Maybe that. And Sylvie says, That's where the medicine is.

She has access to some unknowable energy. Her presence grants me permission to access it within myself. Showing me a door that I alone must walk through. A glimpse of grace that might sustain me. Could be that I am looking for sparkling synchronicity where there is none. Could be the weed.

In the movie of my life, I would buy her bouquets of carnations in all the garish colors—a campy armful that would smell not floral, not really, just *alive*. I'd buy her dozens of dozens, so many she'd have to cradle them in the crook of her arm as a blooming Day-Glo baby. Because isn't that it, the delight in gifting flowers? The look of your dear one as they hold their armful close.

You are the star of the dance recital! We've tallied the votes and you, my dear, are the queen!

Or I'd take her to the Office Depot and set her loose among the fancy markers and the fancy notebooks. With a sweeping flourish, with some bass in my voice for emphasis, I would say: Whatever you want, baby, on me.

It's been a long time since I was certain of anything. Even then—

We should definitely hang out again, she says as she walks me to the door.

Totally.

No, I mean for real.

I mean for real too.

You promise? she says.

I promise, I say, honestly. For once, honest.

READ ALL OVER

Handmade in Brooklyn, the catalog says. Handmade! Brooklyn! I have no way of knowing how I wind up on these mailing lists.

For $135, a golf ball-sized paperweight of faceted glass. *Shattered glass*. For those out there shattering the glass ceiling, the copy reads.

And a silk cord necklace, its chrome-looking pendant the length and width of a pencil. Discreet, the copy reads. Empowering, too. The chrome-looking pendant, a cold metal vibrator. So, if you have the insatiable urge to burn your clit clean off while on the go, well they've got the necklace for you. What a world.

I talk a lot of shit for someone who fell down putting on her underpants this morning. Maybe there's some fight left in me yet.

Copy. Subhede. Pub—short for publication. I throw around these words like they mean something. They're all that's left from my time at the magazine. My tenure there as a copywriter was too short to even consider it a job, even for me. But it was an education of sorts.

I learned about the current state of office protocol and bullshit business casual culture. I learned hell is a meeting that could have been an email. I learned proofreading symbols, which I love. Coded red markings that insist I know better.

I learned just how cruel and cutting I can be when provoked. How I still got it.

Of course I was overwhelmed, of course I was. Before, I barely had an email address—just some AOL nonsense and a Facebook page. As if technology were cyclical, as if I could just will it away. So the job, for me, involved a lot of crying in bathroom stalls. But I took it to the bathroom because I am an *adult*.

The publisher of the pub came into the office once a week, only on Mondays. My boss's boss, dressed like a gin-soaked professor vacationing in Kennebunkport. He'd return my copy gored with edits and take me through line by line. There's some good writing in here, he would say. He spoke of my *idears*. That there is a great idear, that's a terrible idear. And I would nod: Mmhmm, yes, of course, I see that now.

Who was I, what had I become, letting someone in wide wale corduroys dominate me like that?

I had a little desk in a little cube. Make it your own, I was told, and so I did. I printed up some photos I'd found online. Snarling lionesses, their faces sheeted with blood. Tacked them all over the damn place. My muses, I told my coworkers. When people espouse the benefits of curating their space? I get it now.

The help wanted ad specified that ideas were what mattered most, not job experience. Idears. I drafted some mock-up lifestyle-y content, landed an interview, and showed up with pages and pages of pitches. The editor took my word that I knew what I was doing, because I sure seemed like I did.

In the end, when I unraveled, when it all came apart, the editor implied she had been duped. That I misrepresented myself as someone not unhinged.

Get in line, bitch. You don't think I feel the same way?

Days after I'd left the job for good, I remembered the half-empty perfume bottle hidden in my desk drawer. What a field day for her!

Which is more mortifying? That my former boss would find out I wear celebrity brand perfume, or that I purchase discontinued celebrity brand perfume in bulk at the flea market?

I'm positive she's been shit-talking all over town, referring to me by first and last name so as to avoid any confusion. My former boss, my new nemesis. I've got a few.

Really, she should be thanking me. Now she's got her own crazy bitch anecdotes to wow the room at networking events.

You think *that's* bad…, I imagine her saying.

I take comfort in her ridiculous Minnie Mouse-looking dresses, her cheap shoes, and knock-off handbags. She's on my list. She is my list.

That's something I love about hip-hop: the vengeance. Rapping at length about who wronged them, who mocked them and said they'd never make it. They put it on the official record. They name names!

My vengeance daydream consumes me. I, too, am taking names. Showers are for staging imaginary confrontations. My skin is papery dry from hot water; from all the scores I've had to settle.

Elle tells me, I'm sure people will take what she says with a grain of salt. Someone who does that, it's more a reflection of who they are than who you are. And it's not as if it's the first time something like this has happened, right?

Wow, I like how you don't try to make me feel better, Elle.

How many neurons does it take to form a thought? How many neurons does it take to screw in a light bulb?

No need to worry. Thoughts are free, is what the Satanists say.

Aisles of pink and white greeting cards embossed with tea roses. They say Mother in elegant cursive. They say Mom. "Funny Mom" is its own section.

I did not invent this, this despairing on Mother's Day. My tears have a soundtrack, an endless feedback loop. It goes a little something like, Why don't they love me?

If you were to ask my mother, she'd tell you I have ruined one Thanksgiving, two Easters, and a birthday.

Whose birthday? Elle says.

Mine.

How does one ruin their own birthday?

Shrug.

Did you—did you just say *shrug*?

The text message I receive from Sylvie says, LET YOUR FRIENDS HELP YOU. All-caps for emphasis. By *friends* she means her, because I only have the one. I see that, as far as Sylvie is concerned, it's all-caps from here on out.

Well, I'm glad to hear you've nearly vanquished your friend, Elle says.

So we're sarcastic now?

The world appears to me as wholly absurd. I am a stranger in a strange land. These customs make no sense to me.

An old sonofabitch lays on the horn, screams out his car window as I am crossing the street in front of him downtown. A cartoon-looking man hunched over the wheel. Rumpled gray suit, rumpled gray skin, hair standing on end with rage.

It's easy to see myself as he sees me: A conspiracy of the universe, a force aligned against him, robbing him of a rolling right turn.

Oh my god, this must be so hard for you, a voice yells. My voice.

I field calls. It's how I make money now. I have a headset and everything.

There's always someone listening on the line. The company calls it Quality Control. They play back the recording during my reviews, and the feedback I receive is always the same. I shouldn't point out the customer's ordering error as much as I should jump into facilitating a solution. They say, We're a solutions-oriented team. They say *team* often, but I am not part of the team. I am a temp.

What I am most grateful for is this: the twerps in Quality Control never mention how often I say *anywho* when flustered. A lot, is how often.

Social media snooping informs me that Teddy has become a realtor. I'm confident I've had a hand in his making; that I've given him an identity structured around not being like me. It has put him in a starched shirt for life. Block, block, block.

Teddy and Liz had both moved back to Pawtucket before Christmas, before everything went to shit once and for all. Both of them, hell bent on accumulating stuff and debt and raised ranches to prove they are *not* poor. They are adults. But there are more of them than there is of me. So maybe I'm wrong. I have been wrong about so many things.

It's hard to remember that light takes time to travel, that the universe is laid out like a book.

Well, you've got a lot on your mind, Elle says.

One of my parts steps up to the mic and says, You should go off your meds and see how you *really* feel. The rest of my parts, they all laugh that crazy bitch off the stage.

FIRST IT'S THE CROCUSES

Then the tulips and daffodils. I don't know how perennials do it but, honestly, good for them.

I'm back to my old bullshit, finding them all over the place. Sticky notes that say, *Help me see this differently.* I've never thought of myself as a mystic. But here we are.

Rosemary is our volunteer coordinator, they say, but only when asked directly. That is my job title, though I am surely not paid.

I hand out the handouts, I collect contact info, I set up the snacks. But I don't speak much. The Helpline trainings are led by women with business cards, with official sounding job titles and lots of initials and degree signifiers following their name.

I'm better one-on-one anyway. I'm not sure what it is that encourages these women to tell me their secrets.

I don't go out anymore, of course I don't. If I did, like to check out a band or something, I'd just stand around all night, counting. You, you, you, and you, you of course, of course you too. I'm no activist. No one cares what I have to say about the matter. Because a crazy bitch deserves what she gets, and I got what was coming to me—right?

I would, if I could, put my arm around the girl I was, then the young woman I was, and tell them both, It's not your fault—but they wouldn't believe me.

So I know where all the bodies are buried. But those named-names aren't mine to share. They belong to these women. What I do is, I listen. I write down the phone number of the intake coordinator. Call, I tell them. These are people who can help.

I shine at police stations. I show up for those who have called the Helpline with an urgent need. I keep them company. I give them bottled water and granola bars and tissues. I snap at the cops calling her hon, telling her to calm down in their fucking cop voice.

What seems to be the problem? they always say.

I was calm until you told me to calm down, and now I am far from calm, not even in the same zip code as calm.

Add volunteering to the long list of shit I said I'd never do. Then write another list, the shit that turned out to be helpful. Compare the two lists; notice the similarities. Then wonder aloud, How could I possibly think I know anything about anything—about anyone, especially me.

I am running, running in an infinite field of matchsticks. With each step, I ignite a match beneath my bare foot. The faster I run, the faster I burn the hell up. Still, I run.

That's strangely beautiful, Elle says.

It means I am my own karma. Because the judgments I've evolved to make don't have to be right all the time, just most of the time. Just after the last judgment I have made. That, or something else I haven't thought of yet.

As far as origin stories go—mortal wounds—there is nothing left unacknowledged. All that remains is the different ways I relate to them. Ways of being so close to my face I couldn't possibly see.

A fish leaps from the water, high above a crystal-clear lake. Upon returning, the fish notices for the first time the very lake in which it has always swam. The fish describes the water.

I caught a glimpse of something. Not god, certainly. Not that forgone thought-terminating cliché. What I glimpsed was something my eyes had not been trained to see.

Part-fish. I must have been one once. But now I am this pink human.

A memory of a little girl standing over her toys, crying for them. A little girl, standing before the mirror, crying. You must have been a real monster, the girl says.

I was unable to scream when I was a fish.

Because, what, fish don't have feelings, is that what you're getting at? I say.

Don't give me the babe in the woods routine, I say.

But, see? This is what I'm talking about. What I've learned to do is, I excise these conversations from myself and set them aside to be addressed at another time.

Because strong pronouncements should be avoided at all costs. There are no absolutes. Even Lucifer was once an angel.

Roads are closed and cops on bikes abound. The mini mart clerk is openly drinking.

It's commencement weekend in Providence. And, still, death doesn't come for me.

It's not a stretch to say these interlopers are terrible. Parents who don't say please and thank you, complaining about the price of everything, expecting everything for free. High-fiving Chads. A million drunk girls crying on a million sidewalks.

And me, I'm blinded by salmon-colored chinos, navy blue blazers with gold emblems; unfettered expectations, a whole world of possibilities unfolding at their feet on command.

You a student? the bus driver asks. Students ride for free this weekend.

I tell him that ship has sailed.

Meaning?

What I said.

Remember who the fuck you are, has become my affirmation.

So far, it goes one of two opposing ways.

I tell Elle I am noticing beauty. My tone is stripped of sentiment. Because beauty has no argument. There is no counterpoint. And Elle says, How long has it been? Who's to say. There's no way of knowing. It was gone, now it's back. Who's to say, is what I say all the time now. I walk back my own judgment. Judgment, judgment everywhere. Or maybe I am not judgmental. Maybe it's just that I have standards. Maybe I have taste. But who's to say for sure.

Do I—do I like existing?

I wait for things to get easier. They don't. Still, I wait.

Is this hope? Is that what this is? Hope, then, is for suckers because hope has to be replenished. What's required of me is faith. Some method that starts with the answer rather than the question: it will not get easier, no, but you will get better.

Something within me has been clarified.

Elle calls it wizened. I call it impaired.

I imagine my mind as a huge, round conference table, and seated around the conference table are all the parts of me. Every last iteration of myself that has been on-boarded through the years and tasked with a job. Some of these parts think they're the only ones in the room. Some are unwaveringly convinced of their version of the truth, their full and particular account. Some parts demand the total attention of the group, always grabbing for the mic. Some parts are frightened by the shouting, the young ones that want only to feel safe. All of them around the table have a job to do, whether they realize it or not. And every last one of them thinks they have my best interest at heart.

In noticing my parts, merely noticing, I've come to understand how we can bring one another to a deeper sort of completion. The potential to come home to a place we never left. Me and all my parts. There's got to be a way to make the best of all of this noticing I do. And then Elle says, Maybe you should write.

The survivor gets to tell the story, she says, smiling.

I'm gonna tell everyone.

SUMMER

TO WHOM IS THIS STORY BEING TOLD?

Sylvie says, poring over my pages at the kitchen table.
To whom does an echo speak? What would it look like, transcribing an echo?

What does that even mean? she says.

It means, often times, the story of a life told as a story misses the point entirely.

She sighs, chuckles ruefully. Talking to you is like reading the Bible, she says. Sometimes. Other times, I hear you asking the cat how ibuprofen knows where to find the hurt.

I had to read the email twice, and then a third time aloud. *There are some attitudes in this story that the other editors took issue with.*

They called it a cliché, my short story about a young woman—homeless, dreadfully green—and the older street guy who helps her along, only for her to leave him high and dry.

So the world of publishing is, for me, thus far, a world of no. So what? These rejections have no idea who they're dealing with. I like to imagine all the incarnations of my self-loathing filling up a doorway. All of them, telling these rejections: Sorry, you jerks, we're all stocked up here.

Sylvie has offered to cross-reference all the upcoming submission deadlines with my horoscope to see if everything checks out.

And where are we in space and time? Sylvie says. She's holding the manuscript before her like flowers wilted and dying.

Maybe I ought to pepper in some details to orient the reader…

Like?

Like band names are sentences and MTV programming consists of nothing but reality shows about rich kids. Americans are good and plied with energy drinks. The sign of the times? Those gross Hummers in that *Look At Me, I'm a Dick* shade of yellow. A world of shiny, shiny bubbles, shiniest just before they burst.

See. Is that so hard?

In some adapted version of my life, they are out there wondering what secret history I have written. In reality, my vengeance daydream is just that—a dream. This book cannot save me from all that has passed.

It's taking a toll, I tell her. Not just going back there, but inhabiting that state of mind.

And she winces, she blinks her tears in place. All along, I've asked her to approach my stories as works of fiction. Now she's compromised.

I'm never blocked, though; only delayed and, even then, only some of the time. *I'm writing, I'm writing, a few pages of bad writing,* even if I am only writing about having nothing substantive to write about.

And then it springs forth. Like it wants to come.

So it goes, even still, that I can do anything, can withstand anything, so long as I do it every day.

And now?

Now all I want is a room with a door and an ill-gotten Adderall prescription so I can finish this book—is that so much to ask?

Sylvie told me she'd see what she could do.

The heat is oppressive with no end in sight. All of Rhode Island waits for the storm to roll in, to rain down fat rain, to roil thunder and electricity and break up the soup of humidity. The storm doesn't show. Still, we wait like god is coming.

Days pass with cold rinses, lots of them. I rip open the shower curtain. Dot is sprawled in the empty tub and grumbles when I give her the boot.

Sylvie calls out from the kitchen. You know, I really think Dot looks like you. Especially when she's pissed.

Are you joking? Because I've always thought that too.

I air dry before the fan, stretched out on a towel across the floor. If I don't move a muscle I can manage the heat so I don't move.

Never have I ever relocated from one place to another with boxes. Only ever trash bags stuffed to the point of splitting. Like I am fleeing, a thief in the night, and all that. But here they are, stacked all around me, labeled carefully, and raring to go.

Seems to be, I overestimate myself in the Produce Department. I flirt with aspiration. I'm glad for it. A large bowl of nectarines is fast-ripening in the kitchen. The aroma reaches me on the floor where I lay.

Remember. Remember when you would've done anything for all that you have now.

In an effort to beat the heat, Sylvie takes me to see a New Wave film at Brown; a new release directed by the Frenchman who practically invented the genre. You might think, Wow he's still alive?—as we both did.

Is a stereotype still a stereotype when it's embodied by the one who carved out that stereotype in the first place?

For ninety minutes we are trapped, our seats centered squarely in a sold-out auditorium. A small group of solemn-faced faculty members to our left, three breathtakingly stoned graduate students to our right.

I whisper to her, to everyone: Jesus, it's like making eye contact with a stranger while eating a banana. Sylvie squeezes my knee. Like— I'm sorry, I am so sorry.

We start in on it before we've even left the auditorium, both of us cackling. How would I describe the film to a stranger, she wants to know. I tell her the only possible way is this: *Fuhfuhfuh fuhfuh fuhfuhfuhfuh.*

The humid air is syrup and holds our laughter in place all around us.

A prayer I say: remember.

There is no limit to what I don't know. But here is something I know for sure. In my stories, I often write past the ending because I do not trust the reader to pick up on what I'm putting down.

And yet—

Acknowledgments

Thank you, thank you:

Dawn and Andrew
My beloved Hedgebrook
The Karbowski Family
John and Cliff
Lizbeta
The public library, all my bookcase deities

And Bethany
And Craig.

About the Author

CARL CRASH

Courtney Denelle is a writer living in Providence. She received her greater education from the public library. This is her first novel. Find her online at courtneydenelle.com and on Instagram @courtneydenelle

Also from Santa Fe Writers Project

Mona at Sea *by Elizabeth Gonzalez James*

This sharp, witty debut introduces us to Mona Mireles — observant to a fault, unflinching in her opinions, and uncompromisingly confident in her professional abilities. Mona is a Millennial perfectionist who fails upwards in the midst of the 2008 economic crisis.

"Mona at Sea is sharply written Millennial malaise that dares to be hopeful."

— *Georgia Clark,* San Francisco Chronicle

If the Ice Had Held *by Wendy J. Fox*

Melanie Henderson's life is a lie. The scandal of her birth and the identity of her true parents is kept from her family's small, conservative Colorado town. Not even she knows the truth: that her birth mother was just 14 and unmarried to her father, a local boy who drowned when he tried to take a shortcut across an icy river.

"Razor-sharp... written with incredible grace and assurance."

— *Benjamin Percy, author of* The Dark Net

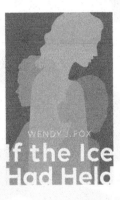

I'm Not Hungry But I Could Eat
by Christopher Gonzalez

Christopher Gonzalez's compact short story collection about messy and hunger-fueled bisexual Puerto Rican men who strive to satisfy their cravings of the stomach, heart, and soul in a conflicted and unpredictable world.

"Gonzalez works multiple registers, creating rich, compressed portraits of his characters. This is as poignant as it is hilarious."

—Publishers Weekly, *Starred review*

About Santa Fe Writers Project

SFWP is an independent press founded in 1998. We publish exciting fiction and creative nonfiction of every genre.

 @santafewritersproject | @SFWP | www.sfwp.com

IT'S NOT NOTHING

COURTNEY DENELLE

sfwp.com

Library of Congress Cataloging-in-Publication Data
Names: Denelle, Courtney, 1982- author.
Title: It's not nothing / Courtney Denelle.
Other titles: It is not nothing
Description: Santa Fe, NM : Santa Fe Writers Project, 2022. | Summary:
"Rosemary Candwell's past has exploded into her present. Down-and-out
and deteriorating, she drifts from anonymous beds and bars in
Providence, to a homeless shelter hidden among the hedge-rowed avenues
of Newport, and through the revolving door of service jobs and quick-fix
psychiatric care, always grasping for hope, for a solution. She's
desperate to readjust back into a family and a world that has deemed her
- a crazy bitch living a choice they believe she could simply un-choose at
any time. She endures flashbacks and panic attacks, migraines and
nightmares. She can't sleep or she sleeps for days; she lashes out at
anyone and everyone, especially herself. She abuses over-the-counter
cold medicine and guzzles down anything caffeinated just to feel less
alone. What if her family is right? What if she is truly broken beyond
repair? Drawn from the author's experience of homelessness and trauma
recovery, It's Not Nothing is a collage of small moments, biting jokes,
intrusive memories, and quiet epiphanies meant to reveal a greater
truth: Resilience never looks the way we expect it to look"— Provided
by publisher.
Identifiers: LCCN 2022005199 (print) | LCCN 2022005200 (ebook) |
    ISBN 9781951631239 (trade paperback) | ISBN 9781951631246 (ebook)
Subjects: LCGFT: Novels.
Classification: LCC PS3604.E535 I87 2022 (print) |
    LCC PS3604.E535 (ebook) | DDC 813/.6—dc23/eng/20220415
LC record available at https://lccn.loc.gov/2022005199
LC ebook record available at https://lccn.loc.gov/2022005200

Published by SFWP
369 Montezuma Ave. #350
Santa Fe, NM 87501
www.sfwp.com

For Bethany, my North Star

And it's inside myself that I must
create someone who will understand.

—Clarice Lispector

SUMMER

THE OLD INJURIES SWELL WITHIN ME

Stories told and retold. They taste like blood in my mouth.

The doctors all say, Well said, and I swallow my contempt at their surprise. I resist the urge to tell them, Yes, of course. *Well said* is my thing. They have no way of knowing it's all I've got left, this describing the water as I drown.

Here I am treated with an exasperated sigh, a port in the arm meant to replenish, a bald turkey sandwich, and a plastic cup of apple juice. No one promises things will get better. No one says this too shall pass. Their only answer to having seen it all before is a neutrality of language with disdain vibrating just beneath the surface. It's just as well. Nothing can be promised to me now. I do not want it to be.

I'm curtained off and left alone, a picture of wrack and ruin. Is this relief that I am feeling or is this dread? Why not both, is what I venture. In that way, the end starts from here.

We had been stopped at the red light alongside Memorial Hospital when I saw them. Gray and withered, outfitted in papery johnnies, gathered together at the main entrance. Each had a cigarette in one hand, the slim pole of an IV drip in the other. Plastic tubes fastened to their arms. Automatic doors opened and closed behind them, a metronome marking time.

I was just a girl then, but the sight of them circling beneath their smoke cloud had conjured an absent feeling in me. Like a dream that reminded me of something I'd forgotten as opposed to a memory of the thing itself.

The dead take their secrets with them.

I don't have to see them to know they're out there. Revenants, all of them. Circling, circling—cast out but unable to cross over, tethered to life. I consider my options. How I could make my way out there and bum a smoke. How I could get out. How I could get on with it. How I could get away.

On the Incurable Ward, the door locked both ways. A door made of steel. But not here. I squeak and wobble down the hall, white-knuckling the IV drip by my side. The whispers at the nurses' station rise and fall as I pass.

There's the world you live in, then there's the previous state of the world the moment you choose to act. Actions and the extension of those actions. They are separate but intersecting circles.